THE UNLIKELY CHOICE

A True-Life Love Story

J. Wreh Dixon

This book is dedicated to my late father, Brown Togba-Wreh Dixon, Sr., who taught me hard work, responsibility, leadership, education, and meditation. His guidance prepared me for life's challenges, and his lessons shaped my path. I hope his soul rests in peace.

I also dedicate this book to my wife, Darlene Adams-Dixon, who has brought love and support into my life, helping me rediscover myself and achieve my dreams.

Lastly, I dedicate this book to God for empowering me with the ability to grow and control my destiny. I am grateful for divine guidance inspiring me to reach higher and live my purpose.

CONTENTS

INTRODUCTION

"The Unlikely Choice" is a true-life love story of a married man whose wife abandoned him for five years and suddenly one evening while taking his usual run on an elementary school wellness track in suburban Marietta, Cobb County, encountered Samantha. The track is widely used by students and the community for exercising.

It was a beautiful hot summer day when Tieh met Samantha and befriended her. Thereafter, their friendship grew and evolved into this bizarre relationship with Tieh expressing his affection for Samantha.

On the other hand, though Samantha was interested in Tieh, she concealed her feeling, introduced, matched, and encouraged him and her best friend and sister she referred to sometimes to go out under the illusion that she was still mourning the death of her husband and not ready for love. She also convinced herself and articulated this plan to others that in this way Tieh would continue to be her best friend and stay within her circle of friends. They both took her seriously and agreed to give it a try.

Tieh and Christine agreed to go on their first date a week before Christine was scheduled to go on a girls' trip with Samantha and friends. Tieh had the date well planned and wasted no time making his move on Christine for he already knew she was interested in him and ready for love. He asked Christine if she would consider going out with him, and without hesitation she responded positively.

Samantha was inquisitive and wanted to know how their first date unfolded. Christine was cautious and provided scanted details. Samantha also inquired from Tieh, and he basically did the same. Suddenly Samantha flipped, realizing that she had lost control and felt left in the cold. Samantha wants her friend Tieh back and reveals her true feelings for him. But it comes a little too late!

Tieh is now involved in a committed, loving, and intimate relationship with Christine and has no intention of looking back or turning around. The train had left the station!

Samantha is angry and her relationship with both Tieh and Christine is now fractured and jeopardized, causing a ripple effect among their circle of sisterhood. This is the story of "The Unlikely Choice".

PROLOGUE

This novel is based on true events. However, the names of all characters, specific locations, and certain scenes have been fictionalized to protect privacy. Some details and dialogue have been reimagined or enhanced for narrative purposes. Any resemblance to actual persons, living or deceased, or actual places beyond the general setting is either coincidental or has been altered significantly to preserve anonymity. The emotional truths and core relationship dynamics depicted remain faithful to the real-life story that inspired this work.

Life rarely unfolds according to our carefully arranged plans. Sometimes, the most meaningful connections emerge from unexpected encounters, and the paths we reluctantly take lead us exactly where we need to be. This is one such story— a journey of love lost and found, of opportunities missed and seized, and of the courage required to make choices that defy expectations.

On a sweltering summer evening in suburban

Marietta, Cobb County, two strangers crossed paths on an elementary school wellness track. Neither could have predicted how this chance meeting would alter the course of their lives and the lives of those closest to them. What began as casual conversation between Tieh and Samantha would evolve into a complex web of friendship, attraction, and ultimately, difficult choices.

When the heart speaks, it rarely considers timing or convenience. Sometimes its message arrives too early; sometimes, devastatingly too late. For Samantha, who was still recovering from profound loss, acknowledging her growing feelings for Tieh seemed impossible. For Tieh who had spent years in the limbo of an abandoned marriage, opening himself to new possibilities required a leap of faith he wasn't sure he could make.

What follows is a story about the consequences of our choices—both those made in fear and those made in courage. It's about the peculiar ways love finds us, sometimes through the very detours we create to avoid it. And ultimately, it's about how the most unlikely choice can become the one that leads us home.

TIEH'S LIFE STORY IN BRIEF

Tieh Brown was born and raised in Liberia, West Africa, where he grew up in a large middle-class family that instilled in him the values of responsibility and leadership from an early age. As one of the older siblings, Tieh frequently assumed the role of managing the household during his father's business trips, especially after his parent's divorce. No brother, sister, or even household workers would make decisions without seeking his permission first, cultivating in Tieh a natural authority and sense of duty.

Tieh shared a special bond with his twin brother Togba, with whom he did everything together. Their father, whom they affectionately called "Papa," emphasized the importance of hard work, having earned his Charter Accounting Certification through self-study and correspondence courses—what would now be called online schooling. Papa introduced his sons to eastern religion and meditation practices and later to Christianity, preparing their minds, bodies, and spirits for life's challenges. Tieh especially gravitated toward his father's discipline of daily exercise and meditation before beginning the workday, a practice that would stay with him throughout his life.

This foundation of discipline and diligence served Tieh well academically. He graduated as valedictorian of his high school class with a post-high school diploma in General Drafting, positioning him to enter Civil Engineering School. Alongside his academic pursuits, Tieh was actively involved in the Catholic Church as a Youth Leader and even contemplated entering the priesthood—though this ambition would not last.

During high school, Tieh began dating his sweetheart, who would eventually become his wife. His academic focus shifted when he encountered Liberia's first computer school system, which sparked a passion that led him to change his major from engineering to business. He graduated with an undergraduate degree in Accounting and Business Administration from the University of Liberia, along with an honored certificate in Programming and Systems Analysis from the West African Computer Science Institute.

This specialized training quickly secured him a position at the data center of the Liberia Electricity Corporation while he continued his studies at the University of Liberia. During this busy period, Tieh also got engaged, asked his father for a plot of land, designed a house plan, and supervised its construction - testament to his ability to manage multiple significant responsibilities simultaneously.

Two years later, Tieh married his high school sweetheart, and they soon welcomed their first son. After graduating from university and as the Liberian civil war temporarily subsided, Tieh and his wife made the difficult decision to migrate to the United States. It was a turbulent time in Liberia's history, with visa approvals rare and unpredictable. Though Tieh and his wife managed to secure visas, their four-year-old son was denied. Facing an agonizing choice, they left their child with his wife's parents and departed for America, intending to bring him over once they were established.

Upon arrival in the United States and settling in Newark, NJ, Tieh joined St. Mary's Catholic Church Newark Choir, initially playing the bongo and later serving as Music Minister for about three years —a role he never imagined himself qualified for. With support from the clergy and members of the congregation, he helped incorporate music from various countries to celebrate the church's diversity, an experience that allowed him to develop his lyrical composition and musical skills.

While he and his wife worked to regularize their immigration status, Tieh taught Religion and Math to middle school students. Simultaneously, he enhanced his computer skills through online education at night, drawing on the self-study habits his father had instilled in him.

Within four years, he had acquired two diplomas in Computer Programming and Systems Engineering respectively. Thereafter, embarking on the arduous journey of obtaining numerous certifications from Microsoft, Cisco, Project Management Institute, International Information System Security Certification Consortium, and later obtaining a Master's Degree in Medical Informatics from Northwestern University. These qualifications opened doors for him in the corporate Information Technology (IT) world, where he steadily climbed from Helpdesk positions to IT Manager.

Tieh's career flourished as he established himself in America, but the separation from his son cast a shadow over these achievements. After three years of persistent effort and legal procedures, they finally secured permission for their son to join them. The reunion was joyful but challenging, as they worked to rebuild bonds strained by years of separation.

By his early forties, Tieh had built an admirable professional reputation in the corporate tech sector, specializing in infrastructure security and database management for a major healthcare system. His personal life, however, took an unexpected turn when his wife of twenty years began growing distant. The arguments started subtly—complaints about his rigid routines, his singular focus on providing stability, his reluctance to take risks. Tieh, shaped by years of responsibility and leadership, struggled to understand her dissatisfaction with what he viewed as his strengths. Concerned about their long-standing relationship and family, Tieh reached out to their Parish Priest who advised that they seek counselling. However, to no avail!

Then one morning, after five years of increasingly strained relations, Tieh woke to find her side of the bed empty. A note on the kitchen counter explained that she needed "space to find herself" and didn't know when-or if-she would return. The abandonment echoed painfully with the earlier forced separation from his son, now an adult pursuing his own path.

Tieh waited, clinging to the values of patience and perseverance Papa had taught him decades earlier in Liberia. Weeks turned into months, months into years. Divorce papers remained unsent as he held onto hope that she would return, that they could rebuild what had been lost. For five long years, he lived in suspension, going through life's motions while his heart remained in stasis.

To manage his stress and loneliness, Tieh returned to the meditation and exercise practices his father had taught him. Every evening after work, rain or shine, he would run the track at a local elementary school in Cobb County. Four miles, exactly one hour, the rhythmic movement combined with meditative focus became his therapy, the one space where his mind could find some peace.

It was on this very track, during a particularly hot summer evening, that chance—or perhaps fate—led him to cross paths with Samantha.

SAMANTHA'S LIFE STORY IN BRIEF

Samantha Daniels was a woman defined by resilience. Born to immigrant parents who had sacrificed everything to give her opportunities, she carried their determination in her blood. Growing up in a diverse neighborhood in Decatur, Georgia she learned early to navigate different worlds, developing charisma and adaptability that would serve her well throughout life.

After graduating from Spelman College with a degree in Communications, Samantha built a successful career in public relations. By thirty-eight, she had founded her own boutique PR firm specializing in nonprofit organizations, work that satisfied both her ambition and her desire to have influence on the nonprofit offerings'. Her professional reputation was sterling—Samantha was known for her integrity, creativity, and unwavering work ethic.

Her personal journey had been marked by both

joy and profound sorrow. At twenty-seven, she married David, her high school sweetheart who had waited patiently while she established her career. Their marriage was a partnership in the truest sense —supportive, passionate, and built on unwavering friendship. For eight years, they created a life together, traveling extensively and building a close-knit community of friends who became like family.

When David was diagnosed with an aggressive form of leukemia, Samantha became his fierce advocate and gentle caretaker. For eighteen months, she navigated the labyrinth of treatments, specialists, and clinical trials, always maintaining hope even as the prognosis darkened. She was holding his hand when he took his final breath at thirty-seven, leaving her a widow at thirty-five.

The three years that followed were a blur of grief and gradual healing. Samantha threw herself into her work, found solace in her circle of close female friends (who called themselves "the sisterhood"), and slowly learned to live with the absence of the man she'd planned to grow old with. By the time she met Tieh, she had reached a place of fragile peace— not ready to love again, she told herself and others, but no longer actively drowning in sorrow.

Running had become her therapy, a way to process emotions and find moments of clarity. The elementary school track near her condo offered a safe, convenient place to maintain this therapeutic routine. And it was here, on a sweltering summer evening, that she first noticed the tall, thoughtful man who ran at the same time every day, his consistency a stark contrast to her own unpredictable schedule.

TIEH AND SAMANTHA'S FRIENDSHIP

The first time Tieh noticed Samantha on the track, he barely acknowledged her beyond a polite nod. For weeks, they existed in parallel - sharing the same space but rarely interacting beyond brief greetings. It was a sudden summer thunderstorm that catalyzed their connection.

Dark clouds had gathered unexpectedly, and rain began to pour just as Tieh was completing his third lap. He spotted Samantha huddling under the small awning of the water fountain, clearly unprepared for the downpour. Without thinking twice, he jogged over and offered her the lightweight windbreaker he always carried in his running pack.

"I live just five minutes away," he explained, handing her the jacket. "You look like you have further to go."

Surprised by the gesture, Samantha accepted

gratefully. Their first real conversation unfolded as they waited for the storm to subside. They discovered that they shared not only a love for this particular track, but also a fondness for classic novels and documentary films.

When the rain lessened to drizzle, they parted ways with Samantha promising to return his jacket the following evening. This simple exchange established a pattern. Soon, they were timing their runs to coincide, starting separately but finishing with a cool-down walk together, conversations stretching longer with each meeting.

For Tieh, these interactions were a revelation. After years of emotional isolation following his wife's abandonment, he found himself looking forward to their talks, to Samantha's insightful perspectives and warm laugh. She brought color into his monochrome existence, challenging his viewpoints and drawing him out of the shell he'd created during those five long years of waiting for a woman who never returned.

Samantha, too, found unexpected comfort in Tieh's steadiness. His thoughtful nature and genuine interest in her words were refreshing in a world that often felt chaotic and superficial. Though she had built a fragile peace in the three years since David's passing, Tieh's presence offered something different—not replacing what she had lost but creating something new that eased the lingering ache. Their friendship grew organically, built on shared moments rather than grand gestures.

As summer faded into fall, they expanded their connection beyond the track. Coffee after runs became dinner at local restaurants. Texts about running schedules evolved into daily check-ins and shared articles that reminded one of the other. Without grand declarations or defined boundaries, they were becoming integral parts of each other's lives.

At home, Samantha's children were the first to notice the change in their mother. Fourteen-year-old Mia raised an eyebrow when Samantha's phone chimed with a text during family dinner, something she had always discouraged.

"Who's got you smiling like that, Mom?" Mia asked, exchanging knowing glances with her younger brother Ethan.

"Just Tieh," Samantha replied, quickly tucking her phone away. "He found an article about that documentary I mentioned."

"Tieh this, Tieh that," Ethan mimicked later that week when Samantha mentioned postponing their usual Sunday movie night because Tieh had invited her to a book reading. "You talk about him more than you talk about the weather."

Samantha brushed off her children's teasing, but their observations weren't unfounded. Tieh had become a regular topic in her daily conversations—his perspectives on books they shared, his unique insights on current events, the quiet wisdom that seemed to anchor her increasingly chaotic days.

Her sister Claire noticed too, during their

monthly lunch at their favorite café in Decatur, not far from where Samantha had grown up.

"You look different," Claire remarked, studying Samantha's face across the table. "There's a light in your eyes I haven't seen in years."

Samantha dismissed the comment with a wave. "It's probably just the new running regimen. Endorphins, you know."

"Mmm-hmm," Claire replied, unconvinced. "And does this running regimen have a name? Perhaps starting with T?"

Flushing slightly, Samantha admitted that yes, she and Tieh had been spending considerable time together, but insisted they were just friends.

"Friends who text each other good morning every day?" Claire challenged, having noticed Samantha's distraction when her phone lit up earlier. "Friends who make you glow like you're twenty again?"

Even Samantha's mother picked up on the change during their weekly calls. "You mention this Tieh person quite a lot," she observed. "When do we get to meet him? He sounds like someone special."

"It's not like that, Mom," Samantha protested, though her voice lacked conviction. "We're just good friends who enjoy each other's company."

But privately, Samantha found herself increasingly aware of how much space Tieh occupied in her thoughts. She caught herself saving funny anecdotes to share with him later, noticing books he might enjoy while browsing bookstores, and planning her week around their scheduled meetups. When Ethan offhandedly mentioned that she checked her phone more frequently on days when Tieh was traveling for work, she couldn't deny it.

The women in her "sisterhood"—the close circle of friends who had supported her through David's illness and the grief that followed—exchanged meaningful glances whenever Samantha brought up Tieh's name, which was increasingly often. During their monthly dinner, her friend Christine, who would later play a pivotal role in their story, gently probed about the nature of the relationship.

"You light up when you talk about him," Christine observed. "I haven't seen that since before David got sick."

Samantha deflected, changing the subject quickly. But later that night, she found herself staring at her reflection in the bathroom mirror, seeing what everyone else seemed to notice—the renewed vibrancy in her expression, the softening around her eyes when she thought of Tieh.

By winter, when the track was often too cold or icy for comfortable running, they had established alternative routines - weekend hikes, museum visits, and movie nights that either one could technically have called dates, though neither did. Their friendship had become a sanctuary for them both, a space where they could be fully themselves without judgment or expectation.

The night Samantha brought Tieh to her brother Mark's birthday dinner was a turning point. She hadn't planned it—Tieh had simply been with her when Mark called with a last-minute invitation, insisting she bring "that friend you keep talking about." Though she'd introduced him as "just a running buddy," the knowing smiles exchanged between her family members told a different story.

"You've never looked at any of your other friends the way you look at him," her brother commented quietly as they cleared plates later. "And trust me, he's watching you the same way when you're not looking."

Samantha denied it but found herself replaying moments from the evening—how naturally Tieh had fit into conversations with her family, how he'd remembered details about each person she'd previously mentioned, how her heart had skipped when their hands accidentally touched reaching for the salt.

It was during this period that Tieh began to recognize his feelings were evolving into something deeper. The realization came gradually, then all at once—watching Samantha animatedly describe a project at work, he found himself wondering what it would be like to kiss her, to build a future with her. For a man who had lived in suspension for five years, waiting for a wife who had abandoned him, these feelings stirred both fear and hope. The thought both terrified and exhilarated him.

What Tieh couldn't know was that Samantha was engaged in a complex internal struggle of her own. Each night after returning from time with him, she would sit alone in her kitchen, long after the children had gone to bed, turning over the same questions in her mind. Was this friendship crossing invisible boundaries? Was she ready for what might come next? Could she open herself to love again after losing David, or was it safer to keep Tieh firmly in the category of "friend"? The calendar on her refrigerator, once organized around her children's activities and work deadlines, now featured more and more entries with Tieh's name—evidence of a shift she couldn't ignore but wasn't sure she was prepared to acknowledge.

Her daughter Mia finally broke the tension one evening, finding Samantha staring at her phone, smiling at a photo Tieh had sent of a sunset from his office window.

"Mom," she said gently, sitting beside her. "It's okay to be happy again. We all like him too."

That simple permission from her child planted a seed in Samantha's mind. But instead of nurturing it, she would soon make the unlikely choice that would alter all their paths—suggesting that Tieh might be perfect not for herself, but for her best friend Christine. A decision born from fear that would set in motion a complex triangle none of them were prepared to navigate.

THE FRIEND

Christine Edwards had been Samantha's closest friend since their freshman year at Spelman College. They had met during orientation week, two nervous freshmen who found themselves seated next to each other at a welcome dinner. Christine had spilled iced tea on her schedule, and Samantha, without hesitation, had offered her own meticulously annotated copy. That small act of generosity had sparked a nearly two-decade friendship.

Samantha was vibrant and sometimes impulsive, while Christine was thoughtful and measured. Samantha charged into life with open arms; Christine approached it with careful consideration. Their differences complemented each other, creating a friendship that had weathered career changes, relationships, and—for Christine—standing witness to Samantha's devastating loss when David died.

At thirty-nine, Christine had built a successful career as a pediatric physical therapist at Children's Healthcare of Atlanta, work that satisfied her nurturing nature and analytical mind. She found profound fulfillment in helping children overcome physical challenges, celebrating each small victory alongside their families. Her apartment in Buckhead reflected her ordered approach to life—clean lines, carefully curated art pieces collected during her travels, and bookshelves organized by subject and author.

Unlike many in their social circle, she had never married, choosing instead to focus on her career and extensive travels. She had visited twenty-seven countries, often traveling solo, finding freedom in navigating foreign cities alone. Christine had dated occasionally—a surgeon she met at the hospital, a literature professor who shared her love of classical music, a tech entrepreneur who pursued her for months before she agreed to coffee—but she never found someone who truly captured her interest long-term, a fact that the "sisterhood" often teased her about at their regular gatherings.

"Not everyone needs to pair up," she would respond with quiet confidence when the topic arose. "I'd rather be happily single than unhappily coupled." Yet sometimes, returning to her silent apartment after witnessing the easy affection between Samantha and David, or later, helping Samantha navigate the crushing loneliness of widowhood, Christine wondered if she was missing something essential.

The "sisterhood" had formed organically over the years—six women from different backgrounds who had found each other through various connections and cemented their bond through monthly dinners, an annual beach trip to Tybee Island, and unwavering support through life's celebrations and sorrows. When David was diagnosed, they had rallied around Samantha in shifts, ensuring she never had to face a doctor's appointment or chemotherapy session alone. When he died, they had organized the memorial service, fielded calls from well-wishers, and taken turns staying with Samantha during those first hollow weeks.

Christine had been the one to restore order to Samantha's home after the funeral guests departed, the one who gently coaxed her to eat when grief stole her appetite, the one who held her through the nightmares that plagued her sleep. Their friendship deepened during this period, evolving into something like sisterhood—chosen family bound by love rather than blood.

When Samantha first mentioned her new running friend Tieh during one of their weekly phone calls, Christine thought little of it. "Met someone new at the track," Samantha had said casually. "We waited out that thunderstorm together. Interesting guy—from Liberia originally."

Christine had made an appropriate noise of acknowledgment, and they had moved on to discussing the upcoming school year for Samantha's children. But as weeks passed and Tieh's name appeared with increasing frequency in their conversations, Christine began to notice subtle changes in her friend—a lightness that had been absent since David's death, a spark of anticipation when checking her phone.

During their regular Sunday brunch at BrickTop's in Buckhead, Christine watched Samantha's face illuminate as she recounted Tieh's humorous take on a documentary they had both watched separately. There was an animation in her gestures, a brightness in her eyes that Christine hadn't seen in years.

"He sounds special," Christine remarked carefully, stirring her mimosa with deliberate nonchalance.

"He is," Samantha agreed, before quickly adding, "as a friend. I'm not ready for anything more."

Christine knew better not to push, but she wondered if Samantha was being honest with herself. The way she described Tieh—his kindness, his intelligence, the comfort of his presence— sounded remarkably like the beginnings of love.

At the next sisterhood dinner, hosted at Marissa's spacious home in Vinings, Christine wasn't the only one who noticed the change in Samantha. As they gathered in the kitchen, ostensibly to help prepare dessert but actually to exchange more private conversation away from the dining room, Andrea leaned against the marble counter and fixed Samantha with a knowing look.

"So, when do we get to meet this Tieh we keep hearing about?" she asked, her tone teasing but her eyes serious.

Samantha busied herself with arranging cookies on a serving platter. "It's not like that. We're just friends."

"Friends who text during our sacred sisterhood time," Larissa pointed out, nodding toward Samantha's phone that had chimed three times during dinner.

"He's having trouble with his son," Samantha explained defensively. "He's asking for advice."

"And he's asking you for parenting advice?" Andrea said meaningfully. "Not a co-worker, not a family member. You?"

Christine watched as Samantha's cheeks flushed slightly. She recognized the signs—Samantha was developing feelings she wasn't ready to acknowledge. Christine felt a small, unexpected twinge in her chest. Was it concern for her friend's heart? Or something more complicated?

The following week, during their regular coffee meeting at Dancing Goats Coffee Bar, Samantha seemed distracted. She kept starting sentences and then abandoning them, stirring her latte long after the foam had dissolved.

"What's on your mind?" Christine finally asked, placing her hand over Samantha's to still the nervous stirring.

Samantha looked up, her expression a mixture of confusion and something else Christine couldn't quite identify.

"Tieh brought me flowers yesterday," she said abruptly. "Nothing fancy—just wildflowers he said he spotted on his way to meet me. He thought I'd like the colors."

Christine waited, sensing there was more.

"And Mark said something at his birthday dinner that's been echoing in my head. He said the way Tieh and I look at each other..." Samantha trailed off, then shook her head. "But I can't, Chris. I just can't."

"Can't what?" Christine asked gently.

"Go there. Feel that. It's too soon, too complicated. David hasn't even been gone four years."

"Is there a required waiting period for happiness?" Christine asked, keeping her tone light despite the seriousness of the question.

Samantha's eyes suddenly filled with tears. "I don't know the rules for this. I never thought I'd need to learn them."

Christine moved to the chair beside her friend and wrapped an arm around her shoulders. "There are no rules, Sam. Just your heart."

"That's the problem," Samantha whispered. "My heart's being reckless. I have the kids to think about. And Tieh's situation is complicated—his wife might come back anytime. And what if I'm just latching onto him because he's kind and I'm lonely? What if —"

"What if you're overthinking this?" Christine interrupted gently. "What if you just allow yourself to explore these feelings?"

Samantha was silent for a long moment, then said in a voice so quiet Christine had to lean in to hear: "I'm scared."

The raw vulnerability in that simple admission twisted something in Christine's chest. She wanted to protect her friend, to somehow make this easier for her.

Then, three days later, Samantha called with what seemed like an out-of-the-blue suggestion: "You should meet Tieh."

The invitation came during their Wednesday evening call, when Samantha usually gave Christine updates on her week while preparing dinner.

"I've been wanting to meet him," Christine replied, somewhat surprised by the sudden suggestion after months of hearing about him. "He sounds fascinating."

"More than fascinating," Samantha said, and Christine could hear the smile in her voice. "He's intelligent, thoughtful, has a great sense of humor, and he cooks! He made this amazing Liberian dish with plantains that even Ethan liked, and you know how picky he is."

"High praise indeed," Christine laughed. "So, when and where is this meeting happening?"

"I was thinking maybe the three of us could have dinner next Friday. There's that new Ethiopian place on Peachtree I've been wanting to try."

Something in Samantha's tone caught Christine's attention—a forced casualness that didn't quite ring true. "Any particular reason for the sudden introduction?" she asked carefully.

There was a pause, the sound of water running, then Samantha's voice, slightly too bright: "I just think you two would really get along. You both love documentaries and hiking. And you both have that analytical mind thing going on."

Christine frowned slightly at her phone. This sounded suspiciously like... but no, Samantha wouldn't be trying to set her up. Would she?

"Sam," she said slowly, "are you trying to play matchmaker here?"

Another pause, longer this time. Then Samantha sighed. "Would it be terrible if I was? I mean, you're both amazing people. You're both single. You both mean so much to me."

Christine felt a complex wave of emotions —surprise, confusion, and something else she couldn't quite name. "And what about your feelings for him?" she asked, the question escaping before she could consider its implications.

"What feelings?" Samantha's response came too quickly. "He's my friend, one of my best friends now. And so are you. I just want the people I care about to be happy."

Christine recognized the deflection but decided not to push. If Samantha wasn't ready to acknowledge her feelings, forcing the issue would only cause her to retreat further.

"Alright," she said finally. "Dinner next Friday. But I'm coming as your friend meeting another friend, not as a potential date. Clear?"

"Crystal," Samantha replied, but there was an odd note in her voice that lingered in Christine's mind long after they'd hung up.

That night, as Christine went through her evening routine—removing her makeup with methodical precision, applying the expensive French moisturizer she allowed herself as a small luxury—she found herself wondering about Tieh. She had formed a mental image from Samantha's descriptions: tall, thoughtful eyes, a deliberate way of speaking that revealed his careful consideration of words. She was curious about him, certainly —anyone who had brought such light back into Samantha's life after the darkness of grief was someone worth knowing.

But as she slipped between the cool sheets of her bed, Christine wondered what Samantha was really doing with this introduction. Was she genuinely trying to create a romantic connection between her two friends? Or was this some complicated way of keeping Tieh close while maintaining an emotional distance that felt safe?

Christine had supported Samantha through the darkest period of her life. She had held her friend's hand through grief so profound it had physical weight. She would follow Samantha into this strange new territory too, but with eyes wide open.

As Friday approached, Christine found herself unexpectedly nervous. She deliberated longer than usual over her outfit, finally settling on a deep burgundy wrap dress that complemented her warm brown skin—casual enough for an Ethiopian restaurant but still polished. She arrived at Desta Ethiopian Kitchen ten minutes early, a habit ingrained since childhood, and requested the table Samantha had reserved.

The restaurant hummed with lively conversation, rich aromas of berbere spice and coffee filling the air. Colorful mesob tables and traditional artwork adorned the space, creating an atmosphere both intimate and vibrant. Christine was examining the menu when she spotted Samantha entering, followed closely by Tieh.

In person, he was taller than Christine had imagined from Samantha's descriptions—broad-shouldered with an air of quiet confidence. When Samantha made the introduction, Christine noticed how Tieh's hand lingered briefly on Samantha's elbow, a gesture that seemed unconscious yet intimate.

"I've heard so much about you," Tieh said, his voice carrying the melodic cadence Samantha had mentioned. "The famous Christine who can convince stubborn five-year-olds to do their physical therapy exercises."

"All exaggerated, I'm sure," Christine replied, smiling. "Though I do have a secret weapon—stickers with glitter."

Their conversation flowed easily as they ordered a variety of dishes to share—doro wat, kitfo, and several vegetarian options arranged on a large communal platter with injera bread. Christine observed how Tieh gently guided Samantha toward dishes he thought she'd enjoy, explaining ingredients and preparation methods with enthusiasm.

"My grandmother would disapprove of me

claiming any expertise in East African cuisine," he admitted with a self-deprecating smile. "But Ethiopian food reminds me of home in certain ways."

Throughout dinner, Christine watched the dynamic between Samantha and Tieh with growing clarity. There was an undeniable chemistry—evident in their shared glances, the way they unconsciously mirrored each other's gestures, how their hands occasionally brushed when reaching for food. Yet she also noticed Samantha's careful maintenance of physical distance, the way she would sometimes catch herself leaning toward Tieh and deliberately straighten, creating space between them.

The conversation meandered through safe topics —books they'd recently read, documentaries worth watching, stories about Samantha's children. Christine found herself genuinely enjoying Tieh's company. His insights were thoughtful, his humor subtle but warm, and he listened with rare attentiveness.

It was during dessert—a honey-sweetened cake paired with Ethiopian coffee—when Christine fully understood what was happening. Samantha excused herself to take a call from her babysitter, leaving Christine and Tieh momentarily alone.

"Samantha speaks of you with such fondness," Tieh said, his expression earnest. "She says you've been her rock through everything."

"She's been mine too," Christine replied simply.

"That's what friendship is."

Tieh nodded, his eyes drifting to where Samantha stood near the entrance, phone pressed to her ear. The expression on his face was unmistakable—tender, wistful, and painfully vulnerable.

"She's remarkable," he said softly, almost to himself.

In that moment, Christine knew with absolute certainty that Tieh was in love with Samantha. And based on the matchmaking attempt, she suspected Samantha knew it too—and was frightened by it.

When Samantha returned, she seemed determined to highlight commonalities between Christine and Tieh. "Did you tell Christine about your hiking trip to North Georgia? She loves the trails there too," or "Tieh just finished that documentary series you were talking about last month, Chris."

The attempts were so transparent that Christine caught Tieh's puzzled glance more than once, though he responded graciously each time. By the end of the evening, as they stood outside the restaurant saying goodbyes, the situation felt increasingly surreal to Christine.

"I'll get the car," Tieh offered, leaving the two women momentarily alone.

"Well?" Samantha asked immediately, eyes bright with expectation.

Christine chose her words carefully. "He's wonderful, Sam. Just as you described. And there's clearly a strong connection between you two."

"Between you and him, you mean," Samantha corrected quickly, though her eyes followed Tieh's retreating figure. "I saw how well you got along."

Christine took her friend's hand, squeezing gently. "Sam, that man has feelings for you. Not me."

Samantha's expression flickered with something complex—hope quickly overshadowed by fear. "It's not that simple," she whispered.

"Isn't it?" Christine challenged softly.

Before Samantha could respond, Tieh returned, and the moment passed. They exchanged pleasantries and promises to meet again soon. As Christine drove home, she reflected on the evening with growing concern. Samantha was clearly using her as a buffer, a way to keep Tieh close without confronting her own feelings. And Christine wasn't sure she could—or should—play the role Samantha had scripted for her.

What she couldn't have known then was how that single dinner would set in motion events that would test their friendship in ways neither of them could have anticipated. How one evening would lead to choices that would force all three of them to confront truths about themselves they had long avoided.

That Friday dinner reservation at Desta Ethiopian Kitchen would become, in retrospect, the point of no return—the moment their separate stories began to weave into one complex, challenging narrative that none of them had planned.

THE
MATCHMAKER

The evening air carried the scent of charcoal and fragrant spices as Samantha's backyard came alive with conversation and laughter. String lights swayed gently in the spring breeze above the patio of her condo, casting a warm glow over the gathering of friends. It was one of those perfect Georgia evenings —warm but not yet humid, the kind that invited people to linger outdoors until darkness fully descended.

Samantha had spent the morning meticulously preparing for this barbecue, arranging clusters of wildflowers in mason jars across picnic tables, setting out colorful paper lanterns, and triple-checking that she had everyone's preferred beverages. Her children had helped, fourteen-year-old Mia arranging the playlist that now filtered softly through outdoor speakers, while twelve-year-old Ethan had proudly assembled lawn games in the corner of the shared green space.

The dinner at Desta Ethiopian Kitchen had been just over a week ago, and Christine's words still echoed in Samantha's mind: "That man has feelings for you. Not me." She had brushed off the comment then, but found herself watching more carefully now, searching for signs that confirmed what Christine had suggested.

When Tieh arrived, balancing a large covered dish that filled the air with an enticing aroma, Samantha felt the familiar flutter in her chest that she'd been trying desperately to ignore for months. He wore a simple blue linen shirt that complemented his deep brown skin, and his smile when he caught her eye across the patio made her momentarily forget the other guests around them.

"I brought jollof rice," he announced as she approached, lifting the lid slightly to reveal the vibrant orange-red dish studded with vegetables. "Made with special ingredients I had my cousin ship from Liberia." His voice lowered conspiratorially as he added, "And there's hot tropical pepper sauce on the side, but I've been warning everyone to approach with extreme caution. American palates aren't typically ready for Liberian heat."

Samantha laughed, taking the dish from his hands, their fingers brushing briefly. "I'll be sure to post warning signs. Last time Ethan tried your pepper sauce, he drank half a gallon of milk."

From across the patio, Christine observed their interaction with quiet interest. She had arrived early to help set up, as she always did for

Samantha's gatherings, and now stood chatting with Andrea and Larissa from their "sisterhood." But her attention kept drifting to Samantha and Tieh, noting the easy synchronicity of their movements, how they seemed to communicate with glances and half-finished sentences that required no elaboration.

"Earth to Christine," Larissa nudged her gently. "You're missing my dramatic story about the airline losing my luggage in Miami."

"Sorry," Christine smiled apologetically, refocusing on her friends. "Just people-watching."

"Is that him? Tieh? The famous running buddy we've been hearing about for months?" Andrea asked, following Christine's gaze.

"Must be. Look at how they move around each other—like they're dancing without touching," Larissa observed.

Christine couldn't disagree. There was a palpable energy between Samantha and Tieh that was visible even from across the yard. She felt a complex emotion rise within her—happiness that Samantha seemed so alive again, yet concern about what this might mean for her still-fragile friend. The Ethiopian dinner had been revealing in ways she hadn't anticipated, and Christine was still processing what she had witnessed that night—the unmistakable connection between Samantha and Tieh, and Samantha's puzzling attempt to create something between Christine and Tieh instead.

As the evening progressed, Samantha made

her way through the gathering, introducing Tieh to various friends with obvious pride. Christine noted how he adapted to each conversation —discussing architectural trends with Marissa's husband who worked in urban planning, kneeling to eye level when speaking with children, showing genuine interest when Andrea explained her latest photography project.

When Samantha finally brought him over to Christine, the introduction was casual, as if they hadn't already met over Ethiopian food the previous week.

"You two remember each other from dinner, of course," Samantha said, her hand resting lightly on Tieh's forearm.

"The famous physical therapist who works miracles with children," Tieh said warmly, extending his hand. "Good to see you again, Christine."

His handshake was firm but not overpowering, his accent melodic, giving ordinary English words an almost musical quality. Christine found herself noticing details—the intelligent depth in his dark eyes, the precise way he articulated his words, the slight calluses on his palm suggesting regular physical work despite his office job.

"The jollof rice smells amazing," Christine commented. "Much better than those plantains you were telling me about at Desta."

"A different culinary tradition entirely," he replied with a smile. "Though both require the perfect balance of spices."

Their conversation resumed where it had left off at the Ethiopian restaurant, flowing easily as they continued exploring common interests— a shared love for documentary filmmaking, a preference for mountains over beaches, a mutual appreciation for jazz that spanned both American and African traditions. Samantha stayed with them initially, but soon drifted away to check on other guests, though Christine noticed her glancing back frequently, watching their interaction with that same expectant expression she'd worn at the restaurant.

Later, as twilight deepened into evening and the string lights became the primary illumination, Christine overheard a conversation that would linger in her memory. She was refilling the ice bucket near the drink station when Carolyn, Samantha's overly forward neighbor, cornered Tieh by the dessert table.

"My niece Julia is visiting next month," Carolyn was saying, her voice carrying in the night air. "Lovely girl, just finished her MBA at Emory. I think you two would hit it off splendidly."

Christine couldn't see Tieh's face, but his posture remained relaxed as he gently declined.

"That's very thoughtful, but I'm not really looking right now," he explained, his tone kind but firm.

Carolyn wasn't easily deterred. She glanced meaningfully toward Samantha, who was across the yard helping Ethan reset the cornhole boards.

"Because of Samantha?" she asked with the confidence of someone who had been observing them throughout the evening.

Christine found herself holding her breath, suddenly feeling like an intruder but unable to move away.

Tieh's hesitation was brief but telling. When he spoke, his voice had softened. "Samantha is important to me," he said simply, neither confirming nor denying the implication.

The significance of what he hadn't said hung in the air. Christine felt an unexpected pang of sympathy for this man who clearly harbored feelings for her friend, perhaps unaware of Samantha's conflicted emotions—or worse, fully aware of them but waiting patiently, nonetheless.

As the evening progressed, the party gradually wound down. Parents collected sleepy children, friends departed in groups of twos and threes, promising to get together soon. As was their tradition, Christine stayed to help clean up, working in comfortable tandem with Samantha as they had done countless times before.

They were folding the borrowed card tables when Samantha broached the subject that would further complicate the already tangled web of emotions that had begun to form at the Ethiopian restaurant.

"What did you think of Tieh tonight?" she asked, her tone aiming for casual but missing by a fraction. "Now that you've had more time to get to know him?"

Christine looked up from the table she was collapsing. "He seems great," she replied honestly. "Intelligent, thoughtful, excellent cook. That jollof rice was incredible, even if the pepper sauce nearly killed me." She paused, then added what seemed obvious: "You two clearly have a special connection."

Samantha's hands stilled on the tablecloth she was folding. The patio was now quiet except for them, the only sounds the distant hum of traffic and the soft chirping of spring crickets.

"We do, but..." Samantha's voice trailed off. She meticulously aligned the corners of the tablecloth, a sure sign she was organizing her thoughts. "I'm not ready, Chris. You know that. And I think—I think he deserves someone who is."

Christine studied her friend's face, illuminated in the soft glow of the string lights. There was conflict written in the furrow between her brows, in the way she avoided direct eye contact. It was the same expression she'd worn at Desta when Christine had pointed out Tieh's obvious feelings.

"Samantha," Christine began carefully, "if you have feelings for him—"

"I care about him too much to lead him on," Samantha interrupted, finally looking up. In her eyes, Christine saw a complex mixture of emotions —longing, fear, and something that looked painfully like guilt. "I'm still working through my grief. Some days it still feels like David left, just yesterday. It wouldn't be fair to Tieh. Or to David's memory."

Christine set down the table leg she'd been

folding and moved closer to her friend. "Sam, grief doesn't have a timetable. And loving someone new doesn't diminish what you had with David."

"I know that intellectually," Samantha admitted, her voice barely above a whisper. "But my heart hasn't caught up. And meanwhile, Tieh is there, being patient and kind and wonderful, and I can tell he wants more. I see it in how he looks at me when he thinks I'm not paying attention."

What followed was a continuation of the strange conversation that had begun at the Ethiopian restaurant. As they moved around the backyard gathering forgotten glasses and plates, Samantha elaborated on her plan—one that seemed even more carefully considered now, as though the dinner at Desta had only been the opening move.

"You saw more of him tonight," Samantha said, straightening a chair with unnecessary precision. "You and Tieh have so much in common. You're both analytical, both love the outdoors, both care deeply about making a difference with your work. And I could see how well you got along."

Christine stopped mid-reach for an abandoned napkin, the implication of Samantha's words now crystal clear. This wasn't just a one-time attempt at the restaurant—Samantha was seriously trying to match them. "Wait, are you actually doing this? After our conversation at Desta?"

Samantha turned to face her, expression earnest. "You're both important to me. You're both looking for someone. Why not each other?"

The idea remained as jarring as it had been when Christine first sensed it at the Ethiopian restaurant. "That's not how relationships work, Sam," she said firmly. "You can't just match people like puzzle pieces because they have complementary interests."

"But isn't that exactly what dating apps do?" Samantha countered. "Look, I'm not saying get married tomorrow. I'm saying give it a chance. He's kind, Christine. He's steady and thoughtful in a way most men aren't. And you—you deserve someone who sees how amazing you are."

There was an intensity in Samantha's voice that gave Christine pause. She set down the trash bag she'd been filling and really looked at her friend, trying to understand what was happening beneath the surface.

"Sam," she asked gently, "what's this really about?"

Samantha sighed, sinking into one of the patio chairs. The string lights above cast shifting patterns across her face as they swayed in the night breeze.

"I can't lose him," she admitted finally, her voice small. "He's become so important to me, Chris. His friendship, his perspective, the way he makes me laugh. But I can't give him what he deserves either. I'm still too broken."

The rawness of her confession hung in the air between them. Christine sat in the adjacent chair, reaching out to take Samantha's hand.

"You're not broken," she said firmly. "You're healing. There's a difference."

"Maybe," Samantha conceded. "But the timing is all wrong. His wife could come back any day. My kids are just starting to feel stable again. And I'm terrified of what happens if I open my heart and then lose someone again." She squeezed Christine's hand. "But if you two connected, he'd still be in my life. We could all be friends. It would be perfect."

Christine felt a complicated mix of emotions wash over her—compassion for Samantha's fear, concern about the flawed logic of her plan, and an uncomfortable awareness that part of her was genuinely intrigued by Tieh. Their dinner at Desta had revealed a man of substance and depth, and tonight had only confirmed that impression.

"Just think about it," Samantha pressed when Christine remained silent. "You'll be seeing him again at my birthday dinner next week. Give him a chance, that's all I'm asking. If there's nothing there, no harm done."

What Samantha didn't articulate—perhaps couldn't fully admit even to herself—was the complex tangle of emotions driving her suggestion. Fear of intimacy after such devastating loss. Fear of risking the safe, comfortable friendship she'd built with Tieh by introducing romantic complications. And perhaps most painfully, fear that she wasn't worthy of new love while still carrying the weight of grief for David.

In her mind, this arrangement would preserve what mattered most—her connection to both Tieh and Christine—while protecting her heart from potentially catastrophic damage. It seemed, in that moment under the string lights with the sounds of night creatures rising around them, like the perfect solution to an impossible problem.

"I'll think about it," Christine finally said, knowing that was what Samantha needed to hear, but feeling increasingly uneasy about the path they were considering. The dinner at Desta had been strange enough, but this deliberate matchmaking felt even more problematic now that Christine had witnessed firsthand the unspoken connection between Samantha and Tieh.

As they finished cleaning in companionable silence, neither woman could have predicted how their lives would intertwine from this point forward, or the painful revelations that would eventually force them all to confront difficult truths. The simple backyard barbecue, following that pivotal dinner at the Ethiopian restaurant, had further entangled the threads of their relationships, setting in motion events that would test friendships, challenge assumptions, and ultimately reveal that when it comes to matters of the heart, the unlikely choice is sometimes the only one that matters

THE FIRST DATE

The evening air sparkled with possibility as the valet attendants welcomed guests at La Grotta, an upscale Italian restaurant nestled in the heart of Buckhead. Samantha's birthday celebration had been meticulously planned by her "sisterhood," with Andrea taking charge of the reservations at this intimate venue known for its old-world charm and exceptional wine list. Candlelight bathed the private dining room in a warm amber glow, softening features and creating an atmosphere of comfortable elegance.

Samantha arrived wearing a deep blue dress that complemented her warm brown skin, her signature silver pendant—a gift from David on their last anniversary—catching the light as she moved among her guests. Her laughter, genuine and uninhibited, carried across the room as she greeted each friend with embraces and expressions of gratitude for their presence.

When Tieh arrived, fifteen minutes early and carrying a small, exquisitely wrapped package, Christine noticed how Samantha's expression shifted subtly—her smile warming, her posture straightening almost imperceptibly. He had dressed for the occasion in a charcoal suit with a subtle blue tie that, Christine couldn't help noticing, perfectly matched Samantha's dress. Whether coincidental or intentional, the visual harmony between them was striking.

"You look beautiful," Tieh told Samantha as he kissed her cheek, presenting the small package. "Happy birthday."

Samantha unwrapped it carefully, revealing an antique brass compass nestled in velvet.

"Because you helped me find my direction when I was lost," he explained quietly, the moment feeling almost too intimate for observers.

Samantha's fingers traced the compass reverently. "It's perfect," she whispered, emotion making her voice catch slightly.

Throughout the evening, Christine found herself repeatedly in conversation with Tieh, sometimes by circumstance and sometimes by Samantha's obvious orchestration. As they discussed everything from the merits of different hiking trails around Atlanta to the latest documentary series they'd both watched, Christine was struck by how easy it was to talk with him. His perspectives were thoughtful, his questions genuine, and his laughter came readily at her dry observations about their mutual interests.

"I've never met someone who arranges their bookshelf by color rather than author or subject," Tieh remarked when Christine mentioned her recent apartment redecoration. "I'd find that completely disorienting."

"It's visually pleasing," Christine defended with a smile. "And I have an excellent memory for which book is which color."

"But what about series with different colored spines?"

"Those get special dispensation to stay together," she conceded. "I'm not a monster."

Their shared laughter drew glances from across the room, including from Samantha, who was deep in conversation with Larissa but seemed acutely aware of their interaction. If she felt anything beyond pleasure at seeing her two friends connecting, her carefully composed expression revealed nothing.

The evening proceeded with the familiar rhythm of longtime friends—shared jokes, gentle teasing, and the comfortable shorthand that develops among people with history. The "sisterhood" presented Samantha with a collective gift—a weekend photography workshop with a renowned nature photographer she'd long admired, scheduled for later in the year. The thoughtfulness of the present brought tears to Samantha's eyes.

"You all know me too well," she said, looking around the table at the women who had supported her through the darkest period of her life.

As dessert arrived—a decadent tiramisu that the restaurant was famous for—conversations fragmented into smaller groups. Christine found herself seated beside Tieh at the corner of the table, both nursing glasses of dessert wine.

"Samantha mentioned you've traveled extensively," Tieh said, turning slightly to face her more directly. "Twenty-seven countries, if I remember correctly?"

Christine raised an eyebrow. "She's been talking about me, has she?"

A smile played at the corners of his mouth. "Only good things. Though she failed to mention you speak four languages."

"Three and a half," Christine corrected. "My Portuguese is functional but not fluent. And what else has she told you about me?"

"That you're brilliant with children. That you once hiked the entire Appalachian Trail solo. That you make the best chocolate soufflé she's ever tasted." His expression grew more serious. "And that you were her anchor when David was sick."

Something in his tone—respectful, almost reverent—touched Christine. "She would have done the same for me," she said simply.

They fell into easy conversation about their respective childhoods—Christine in a suburb of Detroit with educator parents who emphasized cultural experiences over material possessions, Tieh in Liberia with a father who taught him meditation and discipline. Despite their vastly different backgrounds, there were surprising parallels in their values and perspectives.

As the evening wound down, Christine moved toward the restaurant's entrance and checked her phone for her Uber's arrival time. Tieh approached, having just said goodnight to Samantha, who was still inside settling the bill.

"I've enjoyed talking with you tonight," he said, his directness surprising her. There was something refreshingly straightforward about him—no games, no pretense. "Would you be interested in getting coffee sometime?"

Christine felt a flutter of unexpected nervousness. Standing this close, she noticed details she'd missed before—the faint scent of sandalwood, a tiny scar above his left eyebrow, the way his eyes creased slightly at the corners when he smiled. Samantha's matchmaking scheme suddenly felt very real.

"I'd like that," she found herself saying before hesitation could take root. Then, feeling a need for complete honesty, she added, "But I should tell you that Samantha mentioned... well, that she thought we might hit it off."

Tieh's expression flickered briefly before settling into a smile that didn't quite reach his eyes. Something complicated passed across his face— confusion, perhaps, or resignation.

"She did mention something similar to me," he acknowledged. "Does that change your answer?"

In that moment, Christine made a choice that would alter the course of three lives. She considered the genuine connection she'd felt with Tieh throughout the evening, weighed against the uncertainty of Samantha's true feelings and intentions.

"No," she said firmly. "It doesn't."

Relief visibly relaxed his shoulders. They exchanged numbers, and as her Uber arrived, Tieh held the door for her with a gentlemanly gesture that felt both old-fashioned and sincere.

"I'll call you tomorrow," he promised.

True to his word, Tieh called the following afternoon. They arranged their first official date for the following weekend, a week before Christine was scheduled to join Samantha and two other members of the "sisterhood" on a girls' trip to Savannah. The timing wasn't lost on Christine—they would have just enough time to determine if there was genuine potential before she'd be face-to-face with Samantha for an entire weekend.

The days leading up to their date passed quickly, filled with text messages that started as casual check-ins and evolved into deeper exchanges about their views on everything from politics to parenthood. Christine found herself looking forward to these messages, often smiling at her phone during breaks between patient sessions at the clinic.

Tieh planned their date with characteristic thoughtfulness—a morning hike at Sweetwater Creek State Park followed by brunch at a local farm-to-table restaurant. The spring weather cooperated perfectly, offering sunshine and mild temperatures as they met in the parking lot early Saturday morning.

Christine arrived in practical hiking attire—moisture-wicking layers, broken-in boots, and a sensible daypack with water and trail snacks. She was pleasantly surprised to see Tieh similarly prepared, without the over-equipped look of occasional hikers trying to impress.

"I brought extra water and some homemade trail mix," he said by way of greeting. "And a first aid kit, just in case."

"Always prepared," Christine observed with approval. "I've got sunscreen and bug spray to contribute to our survival odds."

They set off on the red trail, a moderate path that followed the rushing creek before climbing to offer scenic views of the small rapids and surrounding forest. Away from the influence of mutual friends and Samantha's orchestration, they discovered a natural compatibility that surprised them both.

"I actually graduated high school at seventeen," Christine shared as they navigated a rocky section of trail. "My parents were education advocates who believed grade levels should be based on ability, not age. So, I skipped seventh grade."

"That's impressive," Tieh replied, offering his hand to help her over a particularly steep step. His grip was firm and reassuring. "I was a valedictorian of my class, with a post-high school diploma in General Drafting before university."

"So, we were both overachievers," Christine laughed. "Though I followed it up with a post-high school diploma in Law Enforcement before deciding it wasn't for me."

Tieh stopped mid-stride, turning to her with genuine surprise. "Law Enforcement? That I wouldn't have guessed."

"My brief rebellious phase," she explained. "I wanted to do something my professor parents wouldn't expect. But working with children turned out to be my true calling."

They paused at an overlook, where the creek rushed below them and sunlight dappled through new spring leaves. In this peaceful setting, their conversation flowed as naturally as the water below, moving from work anecdotes to family stories, finding unexpected connections and shared values.

"My father introduced meditation to me when I was just eight," Tieh shared as they sat on a flat rock, sharing the trail mix. "Most kids would have resisted, but something about the practice spoke to me immediately."

"That explains your remarkable calm," Christine observed. "Even when that group of trail runners nearly knocked us over earlier, you didn't flinch."

"Years of practice," he smiled. "Though I'm not always successful. My son can test that calm like no one else."

The mention of his son opened a new avenue of conversation. Christine learned about the painful separation and eventual reunion, how Tieh had worked to rebuild their relationship despite the years apart, and his current pride in his son's academic achievements.

"He's studying computer science at Georgia Tech now," Tieh said, his voice warm with paternal pride. "Smarter than I ever was at his age."

In turn, Christine shared stories of her most memorable patient successes—the five-year-old girl who took her first steps after a devastating car accident, the teenage boy who regained arm function in time to play in his championship baseball game. Tieh listened attentively, asking thoughtful questions that showed genuine interest rather than polite conversation.

After completing the four-mile loop, they drove separately to Southern Crescent Provisions, a charming restaurant in an old farmhouse that specialized in locally sourced ingredients. Over fluffy biscuits with honey butter, perfectly poached eggs, and French press coffee, their conversation deepened.

"What's your greatest fear?" Tieh asked as they lingered over second cups of coffee, the brunch crowd thinning around them.

Christine considered the question seriously. "Professional failure," she admitted after a moment. "Not being able to help a child who needs me. Personal failure too—ending up alone because I've been too cautious to take chances." She met his eyes. "What about you?"

"Not living up to my potential," he answered without hesitation. "My father sacrificed so much to ensure we had opportunities. Wasting that would be unforgivable." He paused, then added more quietly,

"And losing more time. I've already spent five years in limbo, waiting for someone who wasn't coming back."

The honesty of his response touched something in Christine. Here was a man who understood loss and regret, who recognized the value of time.

By the time Tieh walked Christine to her car in the restaurant's gravel parking lot, something had shifted between them. The tentative interest they'd felt at Samantha's gathering had crystallized into definite attraction. Standing beside her car in the spring sunshine, Christine felt a flutter of anticipation as Tieh moved slightly closer.

"I've enjoyed today more than I expected," he said, his voice low and sincere. "Would you consider seeing me again? Perhaps dinner next week?"

Christine's positive response came without hesitation. "I'd like that very much."

For a moment, it seemed he might kiss her, but instead he took her hand and squeezed it gently before stepping back. The gesture was respectful, acknowledging the potential between them without rushing.

As Christine drove home, her thoughts were a jumble of contradictions. The connection with Tieh felt genuine and promising—his intelligence, kindness, and quiet strength appealed to her in ways few men had. Yet she couldn't completely silence the voice in her head questioning the circumstances that had brought them together.

What neither she nor Tieh had discussed openly

was the shadow of Samantha that hung over their budding connection. Christine couldn't help wondering if Tieh was using her as a substitute for the woman he truly wanted but couldn't have. Tieh, in turn, was grappling with his own complicated feelings—genuine attraction to Christine mingled with lingering affection for Samantha and confusion about her motives in bringing them together.

In the days that followed their first date, Samantha's curiosity was palpable. She texted Christine almost immediately Sunday morning: "How did it go? Details, please! Did you like the hiking trail he chose? Was brunch as amazing as the reviews say?"

Christine stared at her phone, unsure how to respond. Normally, she and Samantha shared everything about their dating lives, analyzing each interaction in detail. But something held her back from sharing the full extent of her connection with Tieh—perhaps intuition, perhaps simple privacy.

"We had a nice time," she wrote back eventually. "The trail was beautiful, and the food was excellent. We're going to have dinner next week."

Samantha's response came quickly: "That's it??? Come on, I need more than that! Are we talking friend vibes or something more? Did he do that intense listening thing where you feel like you're the only person in the world?"

Christine set her phone down without replying, feeling strangely protective of her experience with

Tieh. She would call Samantha later, she decided, and share enough to satisfy her friend's curiosity without revealing the depth of her growing feelings.

Meanwhile, Samantha approached Tieh with similar questions during their next scheduled run, receiving equally non-committal answers. For the first time in their friendship, a wall had formed—thin, but unmistakable.

"It was nice," Tieh said as they completed their second lap around the school track. "Christine is easy to talk to."

"And?" Samantha pressed, her pace slightly faster than usual. "Are you going to see her again?"

"We're having dinner next Thursday," he confirmed, watching her profile carefully. "She's quite remarkable—did you know she speaks four languages?"

"Three and a half," Samantha corrected automatically. "Her Portuguese is functional at best." She paused, then asked with attempted casualness, "So you like her?"

Tieh slowed slightly, choosing his words with care. "I do. Thank you for introducing us."

Something in his tone made Samantha miss a step. She recovered quickly, but not before Tieh noticed the stumble.

"Are you okay?" he asked, concern evident in his voice.

"Fine," she assured him brightly—too brightly. "Just clumsy today."

They completed their run in unusual silence,

the easy rapport they normally enjoyed strained by unspoken tensions.

The week progressed with Christine and Tieh's connection deepening through daily texts and a midweek phone call that lasted two hours, covering topics from childhood memories to philosophical debates about free will. Their dinner date at a small Ethiopian restaurant felt like a natural progression, conversation flowing seamlessly as they shared a traditional meal eaten with injera bread instead of utensils.

"I like how this style of eating creates intimacy," Tieh observed as they reached for the same portion of spiced lentils, their fingers briefly touching. "Sharing food from a common plate breaks down barriers."

Christine felt the warmth of his gaze and the light brush of his fingers like electricity. When he walked her to her car later that evening, the kiss they shared was gentle yet promising - a beginning, rather than an ending.

As Christine packed for the Savannah trip that weekend, carefully selecting comfortable yet stylish outfits for the historic city's spring weather, she received a text from Tieh wishing her a good time.

"Enjoy exploring Savannah with your friends," he wrote. "I've heard the architecture is stunning. Looking forward to hearing about it when you return."

The thoughtfulness of the message made her smile. They had seen each other twice more since their first date, each meeting deepening their connection. Despite the complicated circumstances, Christine found herself falling for Tieh's thoughtful nature and gentle humor.

What she could not have known, as she zip closed her weekend bag, was that Samantha was experiencing an unexpected emotional crisis. As the reality of Christine and Tieh's budding relationship became increasingly clear, Samantha was forced to confront the truth she had been avoiding for months: her feelings for Tieh ran far deeper than friendship.

Sitting alone in her kitchen the night before the Savannah trip, staring at old text messages from Tieh and the antique compass he had given her, Samantha realized with crushing clarity that her elaborate scheme had backfired in the most painful way possible. The friend she had pushed toward Tieh was now capturing his heart, while Samantha was left with the consequences of her own fear—of moving on after David, of risking her heart again, of admitting what she truly wanted.

The irony was bitter: in trying to keep Tieh in her life without risking her heart, she might have lost him completely. As she packed her own bag for Savannah, Samantha wondered how she would face Christine for an entire weekend while carrying this new, painful awareness. The girls' trip that had been planned as a carefree get-a-way, now loomed as a weekend of pretense and hidden heartache.

STRAINED RELATIONSHIPS

The historic district of Savannah welcomed the four women with cobblestone streets dappled in golden light filtered through Spanish moss. What should have been a rejuvenating weekend escape—a cherished tradition among the "sisterhood"—instead became the backdrop for the first fractures in the carefully constructed relationships between Samantha, Christine, and by extension, Tieh.

Christine wheeled her weekend bag through the ornate lobby of their boutique hotel, nestled in a restored 19th-century mansion just off Forsyth Park. The scent of magnolias hung in the air, mingling with the faint saltiness that drifted in from the nearby river. As the concierge guided them to their suite—a spacious two-bedroom with period furniture and a wrought-iron balcony overlooking the park's famous fountain—Christine felt her phone vibrate with another text from Tieh.

"Hope you arrived safely. The restaurant I

mentioned on Bull Street is called The Grey. If you go, try the seafood risotto."

She smiled, typing a quick response before catching Samantha's gaze lingering on her phone. Something flickered in her friend's expression— a complicated emotion Christine couldn't quite name—before Samantha turned away with forced brightness to discuss dinner plans with Mia and Janelle.

On the surface, everything proceeded according to their traditional itinerary. They explored the historic squares, fingers trailing across sun-warmed bricks of ancient buildings as tour guides recounted stories of pirates and Civil War generals. They took a candlelit ghost tour, giggling like schoolgirls at tales of spectral appearances in the city's oldest homes. They enjoyed long dinners with too much wine at riverside restaurants, discussing everything from workplace politics to their latest streaming obsessions.

But beneath this veneer of normalcy, Christine began to notice subtle changes in Samantha. She hesitated before laughing when Christine mentioned something Tieh said, stiffened, almost imperceptibly, whenever his name arose in conversation, and the forced casual tone when asking about their relationship but never looking Christine in the eye when asking.

On their second afternoon, as they browsed a local artisan market on Broughton Street, Samantha held up a hand-carved wooden box with intricate geometric patterns.

"Tieh would love this," she said quietly, almost to herself. "It reminds me of that Liberian artwork he showed me from his father's collection."

Christine felt a peculiar tightness in her chest. "You know him well," she observed carefully.

Samantha returned the box to the display, her fingers lingering on its polished surface. "I thought I did," she replied, then quickly moved to another stall, effectively ending the conversation.

That evening, they dined at The Grey, the restaurant Tieh had recommended. While Mia regaled them with stories of her latest dating disaster—a man who had shown up to their first date with his mother—Christine noticed Samantha barely touched her seafood risotto, despite having enthusiastically ordered it at Christine's suggestion.

"Everything okay?" Christine asked as Mia's story concluded with appreciative laughter from the table

"Just tired," Samantha offered with a tight smile that didn't reach her eyes. "And maybe a glass too many of this Pinot."

Later that night, after returning from an evening riverboat cruise, Mia and Janelle retired to their room, pleading exhaustion from the day's activities. Christine and Samantha found themselves alone on the balcony of their shared suite, the humid night air heavy with the scent of jasmine from the courtyard below. City lights twinkled beyond the park's dark expanse, and somewhere in the distance, a street musician played a mournful saxophone melody.

Samantha swirled the last of her bourbon in the cut crystal glass provided by the hotel, her profile illuminated by the soft glow from the street lamps below. The silence between them had stretched uncomfortably for several minutes before she finally spoke.

"Are you in love with him?" she asked suddenly, her voice careful but strained.

Christine felt her heart skip at the directness of the question. She considered deflecting but recognized that the moment for complete honesty had arrived, whether she was prepared for it or not.

"It's early, but... there's potential. Real potential." She paused, watching Samantha's expression carefully. "I've never connected with someone so quickly before."

"I see," Samantha replied, her gaze fixed on the city lights below, fingers tightening ever so lightly around her glass.

"Sam, I need to ask you something," Christine ventured cautiously, her voice barely audible above the distant sounds of nightlife from River Street. "Did you have feelings for Tieh when you suggested we meet?"

The silence that followed felt alive with tension, expanding to fill every corner of the balcony. A cicada droned somewhere nearby, and the saxophone player switched to a more melancholy tune that drifted up from the square.

"I thought I wasn't ready," Samantha finally

admitted, her voice breaking slightly on the last word. "After David... I convinced myself it was better this way. That I could keep him in my life without risking my heart again."

"And now?" Christine asked, though part of her already knew the answer, had seen it in the subtle signs throughout their friendship.

Samantha turned to face her, with the city lights reflecting in her bright eyes with unshed tears. "Now I realize I made a terrible mistake." Her voice dropped to a whisper. "But it's too late, isn't it?"

The question hung in the humid air between them, impossible to answer without someone getting hurt. Christine felt a sickening twist in her stomach—caught between loyalty to her oldest friend and the genuine feelings developing for Tieh, feelings that grew more certain with each day they spent together.

"I never would have pursued this if I'd known, Sam. You have to believe that," Christine said, reaching across the small wrought-iron table to touch her friend's hand.

Samantha didn't pull away, but neither did she return the gesture. "I know," she whispered, a single tear finally escaping to track down her cheek. "That's what makes this so hard. It's my own fault." She wiped the tear away with an abrupt, almost angry motion. "I actually pushed you two together. God, what was I thinking?"

"You were trying to protect yourself," Christine offered gently. "After everything with David..."

"Don't," Samantha interrupted, her voice suddenly sharp. "Don't use David to excuse my cowardice." She stood, moving to the balcony railing. Below, a couple walked hand-in-hand through the square, their laughter drifting upward. "I used his memory as a shield. I wasn't honoring him; I was hiding behind him."

Christine remained seated, uncertain whether approaching her friend would help or hurt in this raw moment. "What do you want me to do?" she asked finally, the question encompassing far more than just the immediate situation.

Samantha remained silent for so long that Christine thought she might not answer. When she finally spoke, her back still turned, her voice carried a resignation that was painful to hear.

"Be happy," she said simply. "If he makes you happy... that's what matters now."

The remainder of the trip maintained its veneer of normality, but the easy camaraderie that had characterized their previous getaways was notably absent. Mia and Janelle exchanged concerned glances at breakfast the next morning when Samantha announced she had a headache and would skip their planned tour of Bonaventure Cemetery, suggesting the others go without her.

"I'll stay back with you," Christine offered immediately. "No," Samantha insisted with same tight smile. "Please, go. Take lots of pictures for me."

When they returned that afternoon, they found

Samantha had spent the day creating an impromptu watercolor of the view from their balcony—something she hadn't done since before David's illness had consumed their lives. The painting was beautiful but somehow melancholy, the park's fountain rendered in shades of blue seemed to bleed into the surrounding greenery.

"I didn't know you'd started painting again," Christine said, genuinely moved by the gesture and what it represented.

"Neither did I," Samantha replied quietly. Sometimes, loss forces growth in unexpected directions. This unspoken truth hovered between them like a lingering cloud.

The final evening passed in a blur of forced conviviality. They attended a jazz performance at a local club, and the music provided a convenient excuse to avoid deeper conversation. Christine's phone remained conspicuously silent in her purse; she had texted Tieh earlier, explaining vaguely that "things were complicated" and she'd call when she returned.

During the drive back to Atlanta the next day, Samantha rode with Mia, citing a need to discuss work matters, while Christine traveled with Janelle. The physical separation felt symbolic of the emotional distance that had grown between them—a chasm neither was certain how to bridge.

When they returned from Savannah, the dynamics had irrevocably shifted. Samantha's weekly dinner with Christine, a tradition that had survived job changes, relationships, and even David's illness and death, suddenly became subject to last-minute cancellations. Their dozens of daily text exchanges, dwindled to perfunctory responses and practical matters.

Samantha's interactions with both Christine and Tieh became strained, infused with a politeness that was more painful than outright anger would have been. She attended group gatherings with the "sisterhood" less frequently, and when she did appear, she arrived late and left early, always with plausible excuses about work commitments or her volunteer schedule at the children's hospital.

The "sisterhood" quickly sensed the tension, Group gatherings became awkward and everyone felt the weight of unspoken conflict. Andrea, always the most direct of the group, finally confronted Christine after a particularly uncomfortable birthday celebration for Janelle, where Samantha had arrived, presented her gift, and departed before the cake was served.

"What happened in Savannah?" Andrea demanded as they walked to their cars afterward. "And don't tell me 'nothing' because we all know better."

Christine leaned against her car, suddenly exhausted. "Sam had feelings for Tieh," she admitted. "Has feelings for him. I didn't know when we started dating."

Andrea's expression shifted from confusion to understanding. "And she's the one who pushed you two together," she realized aloud. "Classic Samantha —protecting herself at all costs."

"Don't be hard on her," Christine defended immediately. "She's been through so much with David."

"We've all been there for her through that," Andrea countered, though her tone softened. "But at some point, she needs to stop using his death as a reason to avoid living." She sighed, fishing her keys from her purse. "This isn't just affecting you three, you know. The whole group feels it. Larissa is practically mediating territory disputes over who sees Samantha when."

"I know," Christine acknowledged. "I just don't know how to fix it."

"Maybe some things can't be fixed," Andrea suggested gently. "Just lived through."

Tieh, caught in the middle, tried to navigate the situation with characteristic thoughtfulness. When Samantha abruptly stopped their running meetups with a brief text citing a change in work schedule, he respected her space but sent occasional messages checking in on her well-being. Her responses grew increasingly brief, until communication nearly ceased altogether.

One rainy Tuesday, about six weeks after the Savannah trip, Tieh found himself at the elementary school track despite knowing Samantha wouldn't be there. The weather had deterred most runners, leaving him alone with his thoughts as he completed lap after lap, rain soaking through his lightweight jacket.

He nearly missed her standing under the small shelter by the track entrance, her red umbrella a bright spot against the gray day.

"Sam," he said, surprise evident in his voice as he jogged toward her. "I didn't expect to see you here."

"I didn't expect to come," she admitted, her smile small but genuine—the first real smile he'd seen from her in weeks. "But some habits are hard to break."

They stood in awkward silence, rain drumming on the metal roof above them.

"How have you been?" he asked finally.

"Surviving," she answered with painful honesty. "Working too much. Painting again, which helps." She paused, then added, "Christine seems happy."

It wasn't a question, but Tieh answered anyway. "She is. We are."

Samantha nodded, looking out at the rain-slicked track rather than at him. "I'm glad. I mean that."

"I know you do," he said softly. "That's who you are."

She finally met his eyes, her own filled with a complicated mixture of regret and resolution. "I've missed our talks," she admitted. "But I needed space to... recalibrate."

"I understand," he said, and he did. In the year they'd known each other, he'd come to recognize her need to process emotions privately before addressing them openly.

"I can't promise things will ever be the way they

were," she continued, her voice strengthening. "But I'd like to try being friends again. Real friends, not whatever twisted version I created in my head."

Tieh felt a weightlift that he hadn't fully acknowledged was there. "I'd like that too," he said simply.

They didn't run that day. Instead, they walked a single lap together under her umbrella, talking of neutral topics—a book they'd both read, his son's latest academic achievements, her new painting projects. It wasn't the easy camaraderie they'd once shared, but it was a beginning of something new— something honest.

Meanwhile, his relationship with Christine continued to deepen beyond the initial attraction. They discovered in each other qualities they had long sought in partners—mutual respect, shared values, and a comfortable partnership that felt both exciting and secure. Three months after their first date, they spent most weekends together, building something that felt increasingly serious.

"My mother wants to meet you," Tieh told Christine one Sunday morning as they prepared breakfast in her kitchen, moving around each other with the ease of established routine. "She's coming to visit next month."

Christine paused in slicing fresh strawberries, suddenly nervous. "That's a big step."

Tieh came up behind her, wrapping his arms around her waist. "Is it too soon?"

She turned in his embrace, searching his face.

"No," she decided, realizing the truth of it as she spoke. "Not too soon."

The introduction of their relationship to family members marked another milestone, another step away from the complicated circumstances of their beginning and toward a future of their own making.

The ripple effects through their social circle were inevitable. Friends felt forced to choose sides, though neither Samantha nor Christine had asked them to. Gatherings became complicated exercises in scheduling to avoid conflict. The once-tight "sisterhood" fractured along fault lines that had never before been tested.

Larissa, who had been closest to Samantha during David's illness, remained steadfastly in her corner, often declining invitations if Christine was attending with Tieh. Andrea, pragmatic as always, refused to take sides and instead organized separate events, trying to maintain connections with everyone. Mia and Janelle vacillated between the two camps, uncomfortable with the division but unwilling to abandon either friend.

For Samantha, this period was one of painful self-reflection. The loss of both Tieh's friendship and Christine's unwavering support left a void that echoed her grief after David's death. She found herself questioning every decision, wondering if her fear of vulnerability had cost her a second chance at love.

Her conversations with her therapist, Dr. Winters, became increasingly focused on patterns of self-sabotage.

"I engineered the perfect loss," she admitted during one particularly difficult session. "I pushed away the man I had feelings for, directly into the arms of one of my closest friends. It's almost impressive in its self-destructiveness."

"Why do you think you did that?" Dr. Winters asked, her gentle persistence familiar after nearly three years of therapy.

Samantha stared out the office window at the Atlanta skyline. "Because losing someone you never fully had feels safer than losing someone you've given your whole heart to," she realized aloud. "I've already survived the worst loss imaginable with David. I couldn't face the possibility of going through that again."

"And now?"

"Now I'm losing anyway," Samantha said, a bitter laugh escaping her. "But without the benefit of having experienced the joy first."

Dr. Winters leaned forward slightly. "What would healing look like for you in this situation?"

Samantha considered the question carefully. "Acceptance, I suppose. Finding a way to be genuinely happy for them, without this constant ache. Finding my own path forward."

"That's a good place to start," Dr. Winters agreed. "And perhaps rebuilding those friendships, even if they look different now."

The first tentative steps toward reconciliation came unexpectedly, nearly five months after the

Savannah trip. Christine's clinic was hosting a fundraising gala for their pediatric rehabilitation center, and she sent invitations to all members of the "sisterhood," including Samantha, more out of courtesy than expectation of attendance.

To her surprise, Samantha not only came but arrived early, elegantly dressed in emerald green, a small gift bag in hand.

"This is for the silent auction," she explained, handing it to a startled Christine. "One of my paintings. It's not much, but if it helps even one child..."

Christine accepted the bag, emotion making speech momentarily impossible. "Thank you," she finally managed. "It means a lot that you came."

Samantha glanced across the room where Tieh was engaged in conversation with a colleague of Christine's. "He's good for you," she observed quietly. "You've been almost glowing these past months."

Christine followed her gaze. "He is," she admitted. "But I've missed you, Sam. We all have."

Samantha took a deep breath, as if gathering courage. "I've missed you too. All of you." She paused, then added, "I'm trying to find my way back. It's just taking longer than I expected."

They didn't solve everything that night. The path to healing would be neither straight nor easy. But it was a beginning—fragile and tentative, but real.

As summer turned to fall, the three lives that had once been so interconnected continued on increasingly separate paths, each carrying the weight of what might have been alongside the reality of what was. But within that reality were seeds of new possibilities—for different relationships, for personal growth, for healing beyond the fractures of misunderstanding and missed opportunities.

On a crisp October evening, Samantha stood alone on her porch, watching leaves spiral down from the massive oak in her front yard. Her phone chimed with a message from the "sisterhood" group chat, dormant for months but suddenly revived by Andrea's determination to reunite them all.

"Thanksgiving at my place this year. ALL of you. No excuses. Bring whoever makes you happy."

Samantha stared at the message for a long moment, then slowly typed her response. "I'll be there. Just me. But that's enough." And for the first time in months, she believed it might be true.

TIEH AND CHRISTINE'S RELATIONSHIP

Against the complicated backdrop of fractured friendships and unresolved emotions, Tieh and Christine's relationship flourished with surprising strength. Perhaps it was the adversity that bonded them so quickly, creating a fortress of intimacy where they could shelter from the storm of social complications. Or perhaps they truly were the match that Samantha had initially envisioned, albeit with different results than she'd anticipated.

The first major step in their evolving relationship came when Christine invited Tieh to accompany her to a conference in Boston where she was presenting her research on innovative pediatric rehabilitation techniques. The trip represented something significant—their first time traveling together, spending consecutive days and nights in each other's company without the comfortable escape routes of separate homes.

"Are you sure you won't be bored?" Christine asked as they packed for the four-day trip. "The conference sessions take up most of the day."

"I'll explore the city while you're presenting," Tieh assured her, carefully folding a dress shirt into his suitcase. "And I want to hear your presentation. I've only seen the practicing-in-front-of-the-mirror version."

The fond teasing in his voice made her smile. He'd patiently listened to her rehearse her presentation multiple times in her living room, offering encouragement and thoughtful feedback that demonstrated how carefully he'd been listening.

Boston in early November greeted them with spectacular fall foliage and crisp air that carried hints of the coming winter. Their hotel room overlooking the Charles River provided a panoramic view of gold and crimson trees lining the opposite shore, the morning sunlight turning the water into a ribbon of molten copper.

On the second evening, after Christine's presentation had been enthusiastically received, they celebrated at an intimate seafood restaurant in the North End. Over candlelight and fresh lobster, Tieh raised his wine glass.

"To Dr. Christine Lewis, whose brilliant work is going to change countless young lives," he toasted, his eyes reflecting genuine pride.

Christine touched her glass to his, feeling a burst of happiness that was becoming increasingly familiar in his presence. "Thank you for being here," she said simply. "It means more than I can say."

Later, walking hand-in-hand through the narrow cobblestone streets, they paused on a small pedestrian bridge. The city lights reflected in the water below, creating constellations that rippled with each passing breeze.

"I feel like I've known you much longer than I have," Tieh admitted, his arm around her shoulders against the evening chill. "Is that strange?"

Christine leaned into him, considering. "No," she decided. "I feel it too. Like we've been taking parallel paths for years, just waiting for the right moment to converge."

The Boston trip confirmed what they were both beginning to suspect—that their connection wasn't merely the honeymoon phase of a new relationship but something with deeper roots and stronger potential. They returned to Atlanta more certain of each other, the inevitable complications with Samantha and their social circle feeling less threatening in the face of what they were building together.

Six months into their relationship, they had established rhythms that suited them both—weekend adventures exploring North Georgia's hiking trails or visiting small towns like Helen and Dahlonega, quiet weeknights sharing meals and discussing their days over glasses of wine on Christine's back porch or in Tieh's meticulously organized kitchen.

Christine came to appreciate Tieh's reliability and thoughtfulness in ways that continually surprised her. When she mentioned in passing a book she'd been wanting to read, it would appear on her doorstep the following day. When she had a particularly difficult case at the clinic—a seven-year-old boy struggling to regain mobility after a severe car accident—Tieh not only listened to her frustrations but also researched alternative therapies that might help, presenting her with carefully organized information rather than quick solutions.

For his part, Tieh found in Christine the perfect balance of independence and emotional availability that he'd never experienced in previous relationships. She had her own full life—her career, her friends, her personal interests—yet always made space for him in ways that felt natural rather than obligatory. She understood his need for occasional solitude to meditate or work on his engineering projects without taking it personally, and she matched his thoughtfulness with her own brand of care—remembering which tea he preferred when stressed or instinctively sensing when he needed encouragement rather than advice.

The shadow of Samantha gradually receded, though never entirely disappeared. There were moments when Tieh would mention something from his running days with her, then grow quiet, caught in a memory he wasn't quite ready to share. Christine sometimes caught herself wondering if she was second choice—a thought she hated for its insecurity—though Tieh's consistent attention and deepening affection proved otherwise.

"Do you ever regret how things happened?" Christine asked one evening as they prepared dinner together in her kitchen, her hands busy chopping vegetables while he marinated chicken for the grill.

Tieh paused, understanding the layers beneath her question. "I regret that someone got hurt," he answered carefully. "But I can't regret finding you."

She nodded, accepting his answer for the truth it held. "Sometimes I worry that the circumstances of how we met will always be there, like a shadow."

He set down the bowl he was working with and came to stand behind her, gently turning her to face him. "The beginning of a story doesn't determine its whole course," he said. "What matters is what we're writing now, together."

Their connection deepened through such honest conversations about difficult subjects —Tieh's past relationships and the lessons learned, Christine's previous relationships that had faltered before reaching true commitment, and yes, the complicated situation with Samantha. These discussions, though sometimes painful, strengthened the foundation they were building together.

When Tieh received divorce papers from his wife —finally arriving after nearly six years of separation —it marked a significant turning point. As he signed the documents that officially ended his marriage, he felt a weight lift that he hadn't realized he'd been carrying.

"I'm ready to move forward completely now," he told Christine that night over dinner at her apartment. "No more looking back."

The words held multiple meanings for them both. As Tieh's divorce proceeded through legal channels, they began tentative discussions about their future - moving in together, whether they wanted children, where they might want to settle long-term. The conversations flowed naturally, with none of the anxiety or uncertainty that had characterized their previous relationships.

They navigated the fractured social landscape as best they could. Christine maintained individual friendships with members of the "sisterhood," meeting Andrea and occasionally Mia for lunches or coffee, careful not to pressure them about Samantha. Tieh developed his own connections with Christine's broader circle. His natural charm and genuine interest in others helped him find his place despite the unusual circumstances.

The first test of their relationship's public resilience came at Andrea's annual Fourth of July barbecue, traditionally attended by the entire "sisterhood" and their partners. Christine had agonized over whether to attend, knowing Samantha would likely be there.

"We could skip it," Tieh offered, watching her fret over the invitation. "There will be other gatherings."

"No," Christine decided firmly. "We can't avoid

these situations forever. And Andrea's been so careful not to take sides."

They arrived bearing Tieh's famous homemade Liberian jollof rice that everyone had become accustomed to and a bottle of Andrea's favorite wine, both feeling the slight awkwardness that accompanied their entrance onto the back deck where a dozen or so people were already gathered. Christine scanned the crowd instinctively, both dreading and hoping to see Samantha.

She was there, seated at the far end of the deck in animated conversation with Larissa, a glass of white wine in hand. She looked good—her hair shorter than Christine remembered, framing her face in a way that accentuated her cheekbones. She wore a sundress Christine hadn't seen before, its bright yellow a stark contrast to the somber colors she'd favored during her grieving period.

Their eyes met across the gathering, and after a momentary hesitation, Samantha offered a small nod of acknowledgment. It wasn't warmth, exactly, but neither was it the cold hostility Christine had feared. It was, perhaps, acceptance—reluctant, but real.

The afternoon progressed with careful navigation of social circles—Tieh and Christine mingling mainly with Andrea's work friends and neighbors, while Samantha stayed primarily with Larissa and Janelle. The blatant avoidance of previous gatherings had evolved into something more civilized, more mature.

Near the end of the evening, as fireworks began to light up the sky above the neighborhood park, Christine found herself momentarily alone at the refreshment table, refilling her water glass. Samantha approached; her movements slightly hesitant.

"Hi," she said simply. "Hi," Christine replied, her heart beating faster than she would have liked. "It's good to see you."

Samantha nodded, then gestured vaguely toward where Tieh stood chatting with Andrea's husband by the grill. "You look happy together," she observed, her voice carefully neutral.

"We are," Christine confirmed, not knowing what else to say.

"Good." Samantha took a deep breath. "That's... good."

The conversation went no further, Larissa called Samantha over to see something on her phone—but the brief exchange felt significant. Not forgiveness, not reconciliation, but perhaps the first tentative step toward a new normal.

As autumn approached, Tieh and Christine's relationship continued to deepen. They began spending almost every night together, alternating between their homes but gradually leaving more personal items at each other's places—Christine's favorite tea and a spare set of scrubs at Tieh's house, his meditation cushion and specific brand of coffee at hers. They met each other's families during the Thanksgiving holiday—Christine's parents who flew in from Michigan, were impressed by Tieh's quiet intelligence and obvious devotion to their daughter. Tieh's close college friends, who over the years had become like family, welcomed Christine with open arms, delighted to see him so content.

As Christmas approached, they decided to host a small holiday gathering to show their relationship's seriousness. The guest list required careful consideration, and after much discussion, they decided to extend an invitation to Samantha, letting her decide whether she felt comfortable attending.

To their surprise, she accepted, arriving with a beautifully wrapped gift and a tentative smile. She didn't stay long, making polite conversation before excusing herself to another engagement, but her presence felt like a benediction of sorts, an acknowledgment that life was moving forward for all of them.

The new year brought new considerations. Their lease renewals were approaching within months of each other, and the logical next step seemed clear, if momentous.

"My place has more space," Tieh pointed out as they discussed the possibility of moving in together. "But your location is closer to the clinic."

"And your backyard is perfect for gardening," Christine countered. "But my kitchen has that island we both love for cooking."

The light-hearted debate continued until Christine suddenly grew serious. "Are we really ready for this?" she asked. "It's only been ten months."

Tieh considered her question with characteristic thoughtfulness. "Time feels like the wrong measure," he said finally. "I've had longer relationships that never reached this level of certainty. This feels right in a way nothing else ever has."

Nearly a year after their first date, during a weekend trip to the North Georgia mountains, Tieh realized with sudden clarity that he wanted to marry Christine. They had hiked to a waterfall that morning, the spring sunshine filtering through new leaves to dapple the forest floor. Christine had stopped to help a young family on the trail, patiently showing a little girl how to use her new binoculars to spot a cardinal in the branches above. Watching her—her face animated, her hands gentle as she guided the child's—Tieh felt something settle in his chest, a certainty that transcended logic or timing.

The thought didn't terrify him as he might once have expected; instead, it felt like the most natural progression imaginable, as inevitable as the water finding its path down the mountainside.

That evening, sitting on the porch of their rented cabin, the mountain valley spread before them in the fading light, Christine rested her head on his shoulder. "I could get used to this view," she murmured contentedly.

"So could I," he agreed, his arm around her shoulders, the weight of a secret decision heavy in his heart—a promise of the question he would soon ask.

He began planning his proposal, wanting it to reflect the thoughtful consideration that had become the hallmark of their relationship. He visited three jewelers before finding a ring that felt right—an emerald-cut sapphire flanked by smaller diamonds, elegant but not ostentatious, distinctive rather than traditional. He consulted with Andrea about Christine's preferences, swearing her to secrecy even as she squealed with delight at his intention.

He considered various scenic locations—perhaps the elementary school track where their story had indirectly begun, or Sweetwater Creek where they'd had their first date, or the botanical gardens where they'd spent a memorable spring afternoon. But ultimately, he decided on something more intimate, more personal to their journey together.

What he couldn't have anticipated was how the past would resurface just as he prepared to secure their future. Two weeks before he planned to propose, as he was finalizing the details, Tieh received news that would prompt him to reflect deeply on the journey that had brought him to this moment of certainty with Christine.

The call came from an old colleague, bringing word of a significant career opportunity that would require relocation—a prestigious position that Tieh had once dreamed of but had long since stopped pursuing. The timing felt almost symbolic, a test of his priorities and the life he now envisioned with

Christine.

TIEH'S PROPOSAL TO CHRISTINE

The unexpected job offer landed like a stone in the still pond of Tieh's life. He sat in his study, watching the evening light cast long shadows across his garden—the garden where Christine had helped him plant autumn chrysanthemums just weeks before, laughing as they got mud on their knees and making plans for spring bulbs.

The position was everything he had once wanted —lead engineer for an innovative sustainable energy project with global impact, the kind of work that could define a career and leave a lasting legacy. But it would mean moving to Seattle, uprooting the life he and Christine had been carefully cultivating together.

Outside his window, the evening had settled into that peculiar Georgia twilight that turned the sky an impossible shade of lavender. A cardinal —Christine's favorite bird—landed on the feeder he had installed specifically because she enjoyed watching them during her morning coffee.

Christine. The thought of her steadied him. What they had built together felt too precious, too genuine to be disrupted by the ghosts of former ambitions. The opportunity might have been his dream years ago, but his dreams had changed. They now included quiet Sunday mornings making pancakes together, planning weekend getaways to the mountains, and the simple pleasure of falling asleep beside someone who understood him completely.

After a thoughtful evening of reflection, Tieh decided transparency was essential. Over breakfast at their favorite weekend café—a small place tucked behind a bookstore where the owner knew their preferences without asking, he told Christine about the offer.

"It's an incredible opportunity," he explained, watching her face carefully. "But it would mean moving to Seattle."

Christine reached across the worn wooden table, her fingers warm as they curled around his. Through the café window, morning light caught the amber highlights in her hair, reminding him of that first morning in Boston when he had realized how deeply he was falling for her.

"That's a big decision," she said softly. "How do you feel about it?"

Her question—centered on his feelings rather than her own concerns—reinforced why he loved her. Unlike previous relationships marked by emotional demands and expectations, Christine's love was generous and secure.

"Five years ago, I would have jumped at it without hesitation," he admitted. "But now... my priorities have shifted. The work would be fulfilling, but the life we're building here means more to me."

Christine squeezed his hand. "I don't want you to regret passing up something you've worked toward for so long."

"I've been thinking about that," Tieh said thoughtfully. "About how we measure success and fulfillment. This job would be professionally satisfying, but at what cost? I've learned that the space between work—the quiet moments, shared experiences, the connection with someone who truly understands you—that's where real fulfillment lives."

As he spoke the words, he felt their truth settle into his bones. The job offer had clarified what he already knew: his future belonged with Christine.

The finalization of Tieh's divorce also came with unexpected emotions. Though he had long since moved past his feelings for his ex-wife, the official end of the marriage prompted reflection on the path that had led him to this point. If she hadn't left, if he hadn't established the running routine at the elementary school track, if he hadn't met Samantha —who then introduced him to Christine—his life would look entirely different.

"It's strange to think how priorities can change so completely, and how heartbreak can eventually lead you somewhere good," he told Christine as they celebrated the divorce decree with a quiet dinner at home. "I wouldn't change a thing now, even the painful parts."

Christine understood. Their journey to each other had been unconventional, even painful at times, but had resulted in a partnership that felt right in ways neither had experienced before.

With his decision made and his attention fully on their future, Tieh focused on his proposal plans. The engagement ring he had selected—a vintage sapphire surrounded by small diamonds—sat hidden in his desk drawer, waiting for the perfect moment. He had chosen it specifically to suit Christine's elegant taste, spending hours researching ethical gem sourcing and vintage settings before finding the perfect piece at a small jeweler in Virginia-Highland.

His proposal plans evolved beyond the generic scenic locations he had initially considered. Knowing Christine's love of literature, he arranged a private tour of a historic library downtown, working secretly with the curator for weeks to orchestrate the perfect moment. On a Saturday afternoon, under the pretense of attending a special exhibit, he brought Christine to the library's rare book room.

The curator, a silver-haired woman named Eleanor who had become a willing accomplice in his plan, led them through the climate-controlled space where first editions and historical manuscripts were housed.

"This might interest you particularly, Dr. Lewis," Eleanor said with practiced nonchalance, gesturing to a display case containing a first edition of Christine's favorite novel. "We've just acquired it for our collection."

Christine's eyes widened with delight as she approached the case. "May I?" she asked, gesturing toward the book.

"Of course," Eleanor replied, unlocking the case with a small key from her lanyard. "Please, feel free to examine it."

As Christine carefully lifted the book from its cradle, her fingers tracing the embossed cover with reverence, Eleanor discreetly stepped back, leaving them alone among the rare volumes. Tieh watched nervously as Christine opened the book to find the ring box he had hidden there earlier that morning, nestled in a small cavity cut into the pages—a modification made to a replica, not the actual rare book, a detail he had been insistent upon with the curator.

The moment she discovered the ring was one Tieh would remember forever—her surprised gasp, the way her eyes flew to his face, wide with disbelief, then softened with understanding as he took her hand and knelt beside the antique reading table.

"Christine," he began, his voice steady despite the thundering of his heart, "you've helped me write a new chapter in my life when I thought the story was over. Will you marry me and let us continue writing together, for all the chapters to come?"

Her joyful "yes" echoed through the quiet room, followed by tears and laughter as he slipped the ring onto her finger. Eleanor reappeared with champagne she had kept chilling in her office, and they toasted their engagement surrounded by centuries of stories—fitting witnesses to the beginning of their own.

Their engagement brought congratulations from most of their social circle, though the reaction from Samantha was noticeably absent at first. In the months since the Fourth of July barbecue, her communication with both of them had dwindled to obligatory holiday greetings and brief interactions at unavoidable group events. The pain of this continued rift tempered their happiness slightly, though neither discussed it openly.

The engagement period passed in a whirl of planning and preparation. They opted for a relatively small wedding to be held in the botanical garden where they had spent countless Sunday afternoons, focusing on quality time with their closest friends and family rather than elaborate displays. Christine's parents embraced Tieh warmly, flying down from Michigan multiple times to help with arrangements. Her father, a retired English professor, took special pleasure in helping write their vows, while her mother bonded with Tieh over their shared love of gardening.

Tieh's close friends from college and his professional colleagues quickly embraced Christine, relieved to see him so content after years of quiet reserve. His oldest friend, Marcus, volunteered to be his best man, teasing him about finally finding someone patient enough to handle his meticulous nature.

During a tasting session with their chosen caterer, Christine's phone chimed with an email notification. She glanced at it casually, then froze, her fork hovering midair.

"It's from Samantha," she said quietly.

Tieh set down his water glass, watching her expression carefully as she read the message. After a moment, Christine's face softened, her eyes growing suspiciously bright.

The message was brief but sincere, congratulating them on their engagement and expressing regret for her distance. "Life is too short to hold onto hurt," Samantha had written. "I miss you both and would welcome a chance to talk when you're ready."

The olive branch prompted a careful reunion over coffee at the small café where the "sisterhood" had held so many of their gatherings in happier times.

The conversation was initially awkward, weighted with unspoken history, but gradually warmed as they found their way toward a new understanding. Samantha looked different—more at peace than they had seen her since before David's death. She had begun dating someone new, she shared—a widower named Michael. After months of encouragement from her therapist, she'd finally agreed to attend a grief support group, and they met there.

"He understands grief in a way most people can't," she explained, stirring her latte absently. "We move at the same pace, I guess. There's no pressure to 'get over it' or 'move on' because we both know that's not how it works."

She showed them a photo on her phone—a candid shot of a tall man with kind eyes and salt-and-pepper hair, laughing as he threw a frisbee to a golden retriever on a beach.

"The relationship is proceeding slowly," Samantha continued, "but it's helped me recognize that my heart has room for new love after all. And that means there's room for forgiveness too."

Christine reached across the table, hesitantly at first, then with more confidence as Samantha met her halfway, their hands linking in a gesture that bridged the chasm of months of estrangement.

"I'm happy for you both," Samantha told them with genuine warmth. "You belong together. I see that now."

As they parted with promises to meet again soon, Samantha hugged them each tightly, whispering to Christine, "David would have approved, you know. He always thought you deserved someone special."

The reconciliation brought a sense of completion as Tieh and Christine approached their wedding day. The circle was healing, allowing them to step into their future with fewer loose ends from the past.

Three weeks before the wedding, a small envelope arrived addressed to both of them in Samantha's distinctive handwriting. Inside was a handcrafted card announcing that the "sisterhood" had regrouped and were planning a surprise wedding shower for Christine.

The event, held in Andrea's backyard transformed by fairy lights and flowers, was a testament to the strength of female friendship that had weathered its greatest test. As Christine was surrounded by her oldest friends, their laughter and tears mingling as they presented her with gifts and memories, Tieh watched from a respectable distance, his heart full.

Larissa approached him, offering a glass of champagne. "It's good to see the band back together," she said, nodding toward where Christine and Samantha were examining a photo album, heads bent close in conversation.

"It's been a long road," Tieh acknowledged. Larissa smiled, clinking her glass against his. "The best journeys usually are."

As twilight descended and the party continued around them, Tieh found himself standing beside the oak tree at the edge of Andrea's property, watching as Christine moved among her friends, radiant with happiness. The golden light of the setting sun caught the sapphire on her finger, sending prisms of blue light dancing across her dress—a promise of their future, brilliant and beautiful, waiting just beyond tomorrow.

The decision to decline the Seattle position had been one of the easiest of his life, Tieh realized as he watched Christine laughing with her friends. Some opportunities were worth sacrificing for the right person, and in Christine, he had found someone who made even his most ambitious professional dreams seem pale by comparison to the life they were building together.

BUILDING A LIFE TOGETHER

The wedding day dawned with that peculiar Georgia spring light—golden and warm, with the morning mist that promised to burn away into perfection. At the historic Riverside Inn overlooking the Chattahoochee River, explosions of white and pink dogwoods and azaleas framed the ceremony site. Christine stood in a sunlit room surrounded by her closest friends.

"I never thought I'd feel this certain about anything," she confessed as Andrea secured the final pearl button on her ivory gown—simple in its elegance with a subtle lace overlay that caught the light as she moved. The dress, like her relationship with Tieh, was understated yet profound, beautiful without demanding attention.

Samantha, who had insisted on helping despite the complicated history, adjusted the small sprig of blue forget-me-nots tucked into Christine's loose updo—"something blue" that matched the sapphire ring that had become such a natural extension of her hand. The gesture spoke volumes about their healing friendship.

"He's a good man," Samantha said softly. "I see that now, more clearly than ever."

Outside, beneath an arbor woven with climbing roses and jasmine, guests gathered on white chairs arranged in a semi-circle rather than traditional rows—Tieh's idea, symbolizing the community that would surround and support their marriage. His parents sat in front, his father stoic but proud, his mother dabbing at tears that had begun before the ceremony even started.

As the string quartet transitioned from prelude music to a gentle hush, Tieh took his position at the side of the arbor. Instead of waiting at the altar, he had another plan. Accepting the guitar passed to him by Marcus, he positioned himself where all could see. The unexpected sight of the groom with an instrument caused a ripple of curious murmurs.

When Christine appeared at the path entrance on her father's arm, a collective intake of breath swept through the gathering. She paused, momentarily caught by the sight of Tieh—not waiting for her arrival but preparing to participate in it.

As she began her walk, Tieh's fingers found the opening chords of a melody only he and Christine recognized—the song he had written for her titled "The Rest of My Life." His voice, clear and honest without pretense of perfection, carried across the hushed audience, accompanied by gentle guitar and the subtle weave of saxophone played by a musician friend from his college days.

"I'm grateful to the Lord that you are mine. I can't believe it turned out to be true. That you have opened your heart to let me into your life. What a peaceful place to dwell, for the rest of my life..."

The lyrics spoke of gratitude, of second chances of finding love when all expectations had been abandoned. Christine's measured steps matched the rhythm of the song, her eyes never leaving Tieh's as he sang directly to her, as though no one else was present.

The raw emotion in his performance brought tears to many eyes—not from sentimental excess but from witnessing something genuine in a world that often felt manufactured. Even Christine's father, a man of few emotional displays, blinked rapidly as he placed his daughter's hand in Tieh's when they reached the arbor.

The officiant—a former professor of Christine's who had become a mentor and friend—guided them through vows they had written themselves. Tieh spoke of patience and appreciation, of learning that real love wasn't about grand gestures but consistent presence. Christine promised understanding and partnership, acknowledging that their path had been unconventional but perfect in its own way.

"You taught me that timing is everything,"

she said, her voice steady despite the tears that threatened, "and that sometimes the universe gets it right when we least expect it."

As they exchanged rings—his, a simple platinum band engraved inside with the words "Balance and Harmony" in both English and Liberian characters, hers a delicate band designed to complement her engagement ring.

The reception flowed with an ease that reflected the couple themselves—elegant without pretension, joyful without forced exuberance. Tables nestled under market lights strung through ancient oaks featured centerpieces of potted herbs and flowering plants that guests would later take home—Christine's idea to create something lasting rather than cut flowers that would fade.

They shared their first dance with a jazz rendition of "At Last," a nod to the time it had taken them to find each other.   As other couples joined them, Tieh noticed Samantha being led onto the dance floor by Michael, the widower she'd been dating for several months. The man's gentle guidance and the relaxed set of Samantha's shoulders suggested a comfort between them that had been developing steadily.

Later, as twilight descended and lanterns created pools of golden light throughout the venue, Samantha approached them, Michael slightly behind her with a respectable distance that suggested he understood the complexity of the situation.

"I have something for you," Samantha said, pressing a small envelope into Christine's hand. "Not exactly a wedding gift—that's already on your registry table—but something I wanted you to have."

Inside was a hand-written note and a delicate silver bookmark engraved with a quote about second chances. Christine read the note silently, then embraced Samantha with complete openness.

"Sometimes the universe knows better than we do," Samantha said softly as she hugged Tieh next. "You two are proof of that."

The exchange represented the closing of one circle and the opening of another with healing that had seemed impossible months before now manifesting in genuine good wishes rather than mere politeness.

As the evening wound down, Tieh and Christine slipped away without elaborate farewell, preferring to leave their celebration still in full swing—a party that could continue without them, just as their friendships would evolve and endure through this new chapter of their lives.

Two days later, they arrived in Venice as evening fell, the water taxi gliding through lagoon waters turned molten gold by sunset. Their hotel, a restored palazzo on a quiet canal away from the main tourist thoroughfares, welcomed them with Prosecco and a room where windows opened to the gentle sounds of water lapping against ancient stones.

"I can't believe we're here," Christine whispered, standing at the window as Tieh wrapped his arms around her from behind, both watching a gondola drift silently past, its passenger's invisible from their vantage point.

"Together," he added, the simple word carrying weight beyond its syllables.

Their honeymoon unfolded across Italy like chapters in a book they were writing together. In Venice, they got deliberately lost in narrow alleyways, discovering tiny workshops where artisans created masks and glass treasures. Christine's natural ease with people helped them connect with locals despite language barriers, while Tieh's meticulous research led them to hidden gems that didn't appear in standard guidebooks.

Florence brought them art and architecture that moved them to silent appreciation, standing hand-in-hand before masterpieces that had witnessed centuries of human experience. They spent an entire afternoon in the Boboli Gardens, finding a secluded bench where they read aloud to each other from a collection of love letters they'd purchased at a tiny bookshop near their hotel.

The Amalfi Coast offered dramatic beauty and moments of reflection. They hiked the Path of the Gods, challenging themselves physically while being rewarded with views that defied adequate description. In small coastal towns, they lingered over long dinners, discussing their hopes and plans with the freedom that comes from being far from daily responsibilities.

It was during a boat tour along the Amalfi coastline, the limestone cliffs rising dramatically from azure waters, that a stranger's observation captured something essential about their relationship. An elderly Italian woman with elegant silver hair and eyes that suggested she had seen much of life had been watching them throughout the journey, her gaze warm rather than intrusive.

As they docked in Positano, she approached them, her movements careful but determined.

"Scusate," she said with a gentle smile, her English accented but clear. "I watch you together. You have... come ti si dice..." she gestured expressively, searching for words, "a beautiful balance. Like dancing partners who trust each other completely."

Before they could respond properly, she patted Tieh's cheek in a gesture somewhere between maternal and knowing, then disappeared into the crowd disembarking from the boat. They stood momentarily stunned, then looked at each other with recognition.

"She's right," Christine said softly. "That's exactly what this feels like."

That observation became a touchstone for them, something they would reference in the years to come—especially during those inevitable moments when marriage presented challenges. "Remember the dancing partners," they would say to each other, a shorthand for returning to the fundamental truth of their partnership.

Returning home brought the sweet relief of familiarity combined with the excitement of truly beginning their life together. The house they had purchased shortly before the wedding—a craftsman bungalow with good bones and a garden that had potential beneath years of neglect—welcomed them with possibilities rather than perfection.

"I kind of love that it needs work," Christine admitted as they unpacked wedding gifts in their kitchen. "It means we get to build it together."

The metaphor wasn't lost on either of them. They established rhythms and routines that honored both their individual needs and their connection as a couple. Mornings began with shared meditation and mindfulness—Tieh's practice that Christine had gradually adopted, finding it centered her for the day ahead. They took breakfast together whenever possible, lingering over coffee on weekends to plan projects or simply enjoy conversation without time constraints.

Their evenings often included walks that echoed Tieh's original running routine but now served as time to decompress together, discussing their days and maintaining connection even during busy periods. Weekends frequently found them working side by side in the garden, transforming it slowly into a space that reflected both his precision and her creativity—geometric beds filled with riotous blooms, a vegetable garden planned with engineer's efficiency but tended with artist's care.

Their professional lives continued alongside their personal growth. Christine's therapy practice thrived, her approach deepening with her own increased understanding of relationship dynamics. Tieh's engineering work brought new challenges and opportunities, including a promotion that recognized his contributions while respecting his clear boundaries around work-life balance—a stance he had developed only after meeting Christine.

Their social circle expanded and contracted in natural ways. The "sisterhood" remained central to Christine's support system, now including occasional gatherings where partners were welcome. Tieh's colleagues began to see him differently as he slowly opened himself to more genuine connections, influenced by Christine's example of emotional authenticity.

Through it all, they protected the core of their relationship with intentional practices—weekly "state of the union" conversations where concerns could be aired before becoming problems, quarterly overnight getaways even if just to a local inn for perspective, technology-free evenings when work threatened to encroach too heavily on home life.

As their first anniversary approached, the inevitable questions about starting a family arose with increasing frequency from well-meaning friends, family, and colleagues. It was a subject they had discussed extensively during their engagement, both wanting children but agreeing to enjoy their first year of marriage before actively trying to conceive.

"Do you feel ready?" Tieh asked one evening as they sat on their porch swing, watching fireflies emerge in the garden twilight. The question contained no pressure, simply an opening to revisit a conversation they had planned to have.

Christine leaned her head against his shoulder, considering. "I think I am," she said finally. "Not because we've checked all the boxes or because it's expected, but because I can't imagine a better partner to parent with."

Their decision to start trying for a child was celebrated privately between them—a shift in intention rather than a major announcement. Like much of their relationship, it represented thoughtful choice rather than external pressure or arbitrary timeline.

On the morning of their first anniversary, they gifted each other not with traditional paper presents but with custom-bound journals. Christine's to Tieh contained reflections on their courtship and first year of marriage, with blank pages for future entries. Tieh's to Christine held his thoughts as well, but also pressed flowers from significant moments—a chrysanthemum from their garden planting, a petal from her bridal bouquet, lavender from their Tuscan honeymoon.

That evening, over a homemade re-creation of their first official date meal, they reminisced about the unlikely path that had brought them together —chance, circumstance, and even Samantha's misguided matchmaking all playing roles in a story neither could have scripted.

"Would you change anything?" Christine asked, candlelight catching the sapphire on her finger as she reached for his hand across their dining table.

Tieh considered the question with characteristic thoughtfulness before answering. "Not a single step," he said finally, his voice quiet but certain. "Every decision, even the painful ones, led us here. How could I regret any of it?"

As night settled around their home, they moved to the porch swing—now their favorite spot for ending days together—and sat in comfortable silence, listening to crickets and watching stars emerge above their garden. The roses they had planted together after returning from Italy were beginning to bloom along the fence, their fragrance drifting up in the warm evening air.

The future stretched before them with its inevitable uncertainties—parenthood perhaps, career evolutions, the natural cycles of joy and challenge that come with a shared life. But beneath these variables lay the constant they had built together: understanding, respect, and a love that had found its way to them despite detours and complications.

In the gentle rhythm of the swing, matching their movements without conscious effort—like those dancing partners the Italian woman had observed—they embodied the balance they had created together. It was precisely this harmony, discovered when neither was looking for it, that would carry them forward through whatever awaited in the chapters yet to be written.

EPILOGUE

As seasons changed and years passed, the story that began with a misunderstanding and a reluctant first date continued to unfold with unexpected grace. On a warm autumn afternoon, much like the one when they had first planted chrysanthemums together, Tieh and Christine sat on their expanded porch—now wrapped around three sides of their craftsman bungalow, a renovation project they had completed the previous spring. Between them, nestled in Christine's arms, their six-month-old daughter Sofia Grace gazed up at the canopy of maple leaves turning brilliant shades of amber and crimson.

"She has your contemplative expression," Christine observed, stroking the baby's dark hair that curled softly against her forehead. "Already watching the world like she's figuring out its patterns."

Tieh smiled, recognizing the truth in Christine's words. Sofia had indeed inherited his thoughtful nature, often observing her surroundings with a quiet intensity that visitors found remarkable in one so young. Yet she had Christine's ready smile, appearing suddenly like sunshine breaking through clouds.

Their journey to parenthood had unfolded with the same measured intention that characterized their relationship. After deciding to start a family on their first anniversary, they had experienced nine months of anticipation before Sofia arrived on a snowy February morning, entering the world with calm deliberation that the delivery nurse had declared "unusually serene for a first-time birth."

The sound of car doors closing in their driveway signaled the arrival of guests. Today marked Sofia's formal introduction to their extended circle of friends and chosen family—not a christening in the traditional sense, but a celebration of community that would surround their daughter throughout her life.

Samantha was the first to appear around the corner of the house, carrying an elaborately wrapped package that seemed disproportionately large for the occasion. Behind her, Michael followed with a more modestly sized gift and a bouquet of autumn flowers. Their relationship had deepened steadily over the past two years; the engagement ring on Samantha's left hand caught the afternoon light as she waved her greeting.

"Let me see this little miracle," Samantha said by way of greeting, setting down her package to receive

Sofia into her arms with practiced ease. The baby gurgled happily, recognizing a face she had seen regularly since her birth.

Michael hung back slightly, still sometimes uncertain of his place in this complicated web of relationships, though everyone had long since welcomed him warmly. "She's grown even in the two weeks since we saw her last," he observed, his voice gentle with wonder.

Soon the garden filled with others—Andrea and Larissa arriving together, bringing handmade gifts and cheerful energy; Marcus and his new wife Jennifer contributing sophisticated cocktails for the adults and a hand-carved wooden rattle for Sofia; Tieh's colleagues from the engineering firm where he now led the sustainable energy IT division; Christine's fellow therapists and clients-turned-friends; even Christine's parents who had relocated to a retirement community just thirty minutes away, drawn by the magnetic pull of their only grandchild.

Notable among the arrivals was Tieh's twin brother Togba, who had flown in from Liberia where he had been managing their family's business interests. His visit carried bittersweet undertones; their father's health had been declining, creating complex conversations about family obligations across continents that would require navigation in the months ahead.

As afternoon eased into evening, lanterns illuminated the garden - the same ones that had lit their wedding reception, now permanently installed along garden paths that wound through beds of herbs and flowers. Sofia was passed from loving arms to loving arms, absorbing the energy and affection of the community her parents had built around them.

Later, when most guests had departed and only the closest circle remained, they gathered around the fire pit Tieh had designed and built during Christine's pregnancy. Sofia slept peacefully in a portable bassinet nearby, monitored by both high-tech baby monitors and the watchful eyes of multiple adults who each felt personal investment in her wellbeing.

"I'd like to offer a toast," Samantha said suddenly, raising her glass of wine. Her voice carried with the confidence she had regained over the past years—a strength different from her former brittle determination, now grounded in genuine self-awareness. "To Sofia, who represents all the unexpected turns life takes us on. And to unlikely choices."

The phrase caught Tieh's attention, stirring memories of the complicated path that had led them all here. As glasses clinked and conversations resumed, he found himself reflecting on the transformative journey each of them had taken.

"The Unlikely Choice" was ultimately a story about how life rarely follows carefully constructed plans, and how what seems like a detour often leads precisely where we need to be. For Tieh, Samantha, and Christine, the journey had been complicated by misunderstandings, timing, and unspoken feelings —yet resulted in connections that transformed each of their lives in necessary ways.

Tieh's marriage to Christine gave him the partnership he had always sought—equal, respectful, and built on genuine compatibility rather than convenience or familiarity. His friendship with Samantha, though transformed from its original form, remained a valued part of his life, a reminder of the unexpected ways people enter our lives and change our trajectories.

For Christine, the relationship brought partnership with a man who valued her independence and strength while offering the steady presence she had never found in previous relationships. The complicated beginnings of their connection had faded in importance compared to the life they were building together—a life filled with mutual respect, shared dreams, and the kind of deep understanding that comes only when two people truly see each other.

Samantha's journey was perhaps the most profound. Her well-intentioned but misguided attempt to keep Tieh in her life while protecting her heart had led to painful revelations about her own readiness for love after loss. Through the process of letting go - of both Tieh and her fears-she found the courage to open herself to new possibilities. Her relationship with Michael developed with a newfound honesty about her needs and vulnerabilities, strengthened by the lessons learned through her friendship with Tieh.

As the evening deepened and stars appeared above their garden, Tieh excused himself briefly, returning with a small wooden box that Christine recognized immediately-the handcrafted container where they kept mementos of significant moments in their relationship.

"I think tonight calls for a new addition," he explained, opening the box to reveal its treasures: the receipt from their first coffee meeting, pressed flowers from various occasions, the cork from the champagne they'd shared after his proposal, a small vial of Italian sand from their honeymoon. From his pocket, he withdrew a small envelope, sealed but unmarked.

"What's this?" Christine asked as he placed it in the box alongside their other memories.

"A letter to Sofia," he explained. "About how she came to be surrounded by so many people who love her-about the unlikely path that created her family." His eyes moved meaningfully around the circle, including not just Christine but Samantha, Michael, and the others who had become integral to their shared story. "I thought we might all write something for her to read someday."

The idea resonated, sparking a conversation about legacies and lessons learned. As paper was distributed and pens uncapped, Togba spoke up from his place beside the fire.

"In our culture, there is a belief that children

are born knowing who will love them," he said, his voice carrying the cadence of their father's. "They choose their path before birth, selecting the precise moment and constellation of people needed for their journey."

The concept settled over the gathering like a blessing. Sofia had indeed arrived into a unique configuration of relationships-bonds formed through difficulty but sustained by genuine care and respect. What had once been a triangle of tension had evolved into an expanded family of choice, each connection adding dimension and richness to the whole.

Life continued to present its challenges. Tieh's father's declining health prompted difficult conversations about international moves and cultural expectations. Christine's recent invitation to join a prestigious counseling center as director brought opportunities that required careful negotiation of their shared responsibilities. Samantha and Michael navigated the complexities of blending their lives as their wedding approached, with Michael's teenage children from his previous marriage adding complexity to their new beginning.

Yet through it all, the foundation remained-three lives forever changed by unexpected connections, by choices made in moments of vulnerability, by the courage to accept that sometimes the path to happiness looks nothing like we imagined.

"The unlikely choice is often the right one," Tieh reflected as he penned his letter to Sofia. "We just have to be brave enough to recognize it."

His thoughts were interrupted by Sofia's soft cries as she awakened. Christine moved to attend to her, but Samantha was already there, lifting the baby with practiced gentleness. "I've got her," she said, her eyes meeting Christine's with understanding that transcended their complicated history.

As Sofia settled against Samantha's shoulder, Michael watched with the tender expression of a man who had found unexpected joy in expanded definitions of family.

Nearby, Togba engaged with Christine's father in animated conversation about international business practices, their cultural differences bridged by mutual respect and shared interests. Andrea and Larissa huddled with Christine's mother, exchanging recipes and gardening tips with the easy camaraderie of women who had discovered common ground despite different life paths.

Looking around at this intricate web of relationships-none of which would exist in this form had events unfolded differently-Tieh felt profound gratitude for all the missteps and detours that had led here. In this gathering of unlikely connections, he saw not just his past and present, but Sofia's future: rich with diverse perspectives, strengthened by people who had learned that love expands rather than diminishes when hearts remain open to possibility.

In this story of love, friendship, and growth, perhaps the most profound lesson was that their hearts had known what they needed long before their minds caught up to the truth. For Tieh, Christine, and Samantha, the winding path of their connection-with all its pain and joy-had led exactly where each needed to be. Not despite the unlikely nature of their choices, but because of them.

As evening deepened into night and conversation continued around the fire, Sofia was passed back to Christine's arms. The baby's eyes, wide and observant, moved from face to beloved face, seeming to catalog the unique constellation of people who formed her world. Tieh watched his daughter's expressions shift with each new discovery, recognizing in her the same curiosity that had led him to take a chance on coffee with Christine, despite all logical reasons not to.

Already, at six months old, Sofia seemed to understand something essential about the improbable beauty of human connection. Perhaps Togba was right-perhaps she had chosen them all, intuiting that this particular tapestry of relationships, with all its complicated threads and unexpected patterns, was precisely where she belonged.

And in that moment, under stars that had witnessed countless human stories unfold, surrounded by the family they had created not through conventional paths but through courage and forgiveness and growth, the circle felt complete. Not perfect-never perfect-but whole in all the ways that truly matter.

ACKNOWLEDGEMENT

I would like to extend my deepest gratitude to Tobyette Wheeler for her exceptional editing work on this book. Tobyette's meticulous attention to detail, insightful suggestions, and unwavering dedication have truly elevated the quality of this manuscript. Her keen eye and thoughtful feedback helped shape this work into its final form, and her support throughout this process has been invaluable.

Thank you, Tobyette, for your remarkable expertise and for being an integral part of this journey.

ABOUT THE AUTHOR

J. Wreh Dixon

J. Wreh Dixon is an IT Engineer and Cybersecurity Professional whose creative spirit extends well beyond the digital realm. As a dedicated Music Minister, he brings his passion for composition to life through religious and romantic songs. When not immersed in technology or music, J. Wreh finds balance through meditation, mindfulness practices, and regular exercise. He treasures time spent with his wife, family, and friends, drawing inspiration for his storytelling from the authentic connections that enrich his life. "The Unlikely Choice" is influenced by his belief in the transformative power of human relationships and the unexpected paths that lead us to where we're meant to be.

Website: www.jwrehdixon.com

THE UNLIKELY CHOICE

What began as a chance encounter on an elementary school wellness track forever altered the lives of Tieh, Samantha, and Christine.

Tieh, still reeling from being abandoned by his wife, finds unexpected comfort in Samantha—a woman quietly grieving her late husband. When Tieh confesses his feelings, Samantha, afraid of reopening old wounds, urges him to date her sister, Christine, instead.

She never imagined they would form a deep, authentic bond—rooted in mutual respect and shared hopes for the future. By the time Samantha realizes her own heart's truth, it's too late. She must now confront the pain of missed timing and the fragile courage it takes to love again.

"The Unlikely Choice" is a tender, emotionally rich story about healing, second chances, and learning to embrace happiness when it arrives in the most unexpected way.